As she and Phil put the finishing touches on the Christmas lights, she jumped at his touch.

"Sorry," she said, as electricity powered through her veins.

"You seem a bit flinchy," he said, drilling her with a stare.

"I'm just a little uptight, with all the new patients and work and all."

Phil lowered his voice and lifted her hair, hooking it behind one ear. "It's Christmastime, pretty baby, loosen up. You know, a little TLC might be just the thing you need."

A vision of tender loving care, compliments of Phil, whirled through her mind. She couldn't breathe for a second. He seemed to know exactly what she'd been thinking, and now her cheeks were probably betraying her by blushing hot pink.

Why not? Was she such a wretched person that she didn't deserve a little pleasure in life?

How many times did she need to give herself permission to live?

Her cheeks flamed and her palms tingled just at her thinking about it. Slowly she glanced into his darkening and decidedly sexy stare.

"I owe you that dinner out. What about tonight?"

What about tonight? She knew what he meant, what he wanted.

So strong was her physical reaction that if everything else could just disappear she'd be on him, knocking him down and ripping off his clothes right this instant.

Nearly trembling with desire, she found her voice, if only a whisper. "Yes. Tonight."

Dear Reader

The Christmas season is a special time of year. Ideally, it is a time of happiness and goodwill towards others. With that in mind, I was hesitant to give my lovely Stephanie Bennett such a difficult and haunting past to overcome. As for carefree Phil Hansen—well, it just seemed cruel to put him through such an emotional rollercoaster by simultaneously dropping two not-so-perfect people into his life. However…I'm a writer, and it is my job to make life miserable for my characters, so with my editor's blessing I laid it on thick in THE CHRISTMAS BABY BUMP.

Stephanie needs a change of scenery for the holidays, and Phil is coerced into filling in as a caregiver for his preschool-aged half-brother. Unbeknownst to both Stephanie and Phil, these two story elements are the perfect ingredients for a Christmas miracle in the making.

Stephanie has an issue she must face and deal with before she can ever hope to find peace of mind and her fair share of happiness. Fortunately Phil, though at first seeming the least likely, is just the man to help her conquer her past.

I hope you enjoy this Santa Barbara Christmas story, the wrap-up book for my MidCoast medical trilogy: THE BOSS AND NURSE ALBRIGHT, THE HEART DOCTOR AND THE BABY and THE CHRISTMAS BABY BUMP. I've grown to love my imaginary friends at the clinic, and I'm so happy I could help them all find their happy-ever-afters.

Lynne
www.lynnemarshall.com

THE CHRISTMAS BABY BUMP

BY
LYNNE MARSHALL

MILLS
BOON

First published in Great Britain 2010
by Mills & Boon,
an imprint of Harlequin (UK) Limited,
Large Print edition 2011
Eton House, 18-24 Paradise Road,
Richmond, Surrey TW9 1SR

© Janet Maarschalk 2010

ISBN: 978 0 263 21735 3

Harlequin (UK) policy is to use papers that are
natural, renewable and recyclable products and made
from wood grown in sustainable forests. The logging
and manufacturing process conform to the legal
environmental regulations of the country of origin.

Printed and bound in Great Britain
by CPI Antony Rowe, Chippenham, Wiltshire

Lynne Marshall has been a Registered Nurse in a large California hospital for twenty-five years. She has now taken the leap to writing full time, but still volunteers at her local community hospital. After writing the book of her heart in 2000, she discovered the wonderful world of Mills & Boon® Medical™ Romance, where she feels the freedom to write the stories she loves. She is happily married, has two fantastic grown children, and a socially challenged rescued dog. Besides her passion for writing Medical Romance, she loves to travel and read. Thanks to the family dog, she takes long walks every day! To find out more about Lynne, please visit her website www.lynnemarshallweb.com

Special thanks to Sally Williamson
for her constant support and
for keeping me on the right path with this story.

CHAPTER ONE

MONDAY morning, Stephanie opened the door of the cream-colored Victorian mansion and headed toward the reception desk. Though the house had been turned into a medical clinic, they'd kept the turn-of-the-century charm. Hardwood floors, tray ceilings, crown molding, wall sconces, even a chandelier made everything feel special. She could get used to showing up for work here.

A man with longish dark blond hair in a suit chatted with not one but two nurses at the receptionist's desk. Nothing short of adoration gleamed from the women's eyes. He looked typical trendy Santa Barbaran—businessman by day in a tailored suit and carefully chosen shirt/tie combo, outdoorsman on the weekends by the tone of his tan. Not bad, if you liked the type.

"Of course I'll help you out, Dr. Hansen," one of the young and attractive nurses gushed.

"Great." He held a clipboard. "I'll pencil you in right here. Anyone else?"

Was he taking advantage of the staff? Unscrupulous.

"Sign me up for Saturday," the middle-aged, magenta-haired receptionist chimed in.

Hmm.

"Got it." As he scribbled in her name his gaze drifted upward. The warm and inviting smile that followed stopped Stephanie in her tracks.

"May I help you?" he said.

Flustered, and not understanding why—okay, she knew exactly why, the guy was gorgeous—she cleared her throat. "I'm Stephanie Bennett. I have an appointment with Dr. Rogers."

"Yes," the older receptionist said, back to all-business. "He's expecting you, Dr. Bennett. I'll let him know you're here."

Before she could take a seat in the waiting room, the man with the bronze-toned suntan (even though it was November!) offered his hand. "I'm

Phil Hansen, the pulmonologist of the group. If you'd like, I'll take you up to Jason's office."

"It's nice to meet you," she said, out of habit.

A long-forgotten feeling twined through her center as she shook his hand. She stiffened. Tingles spiraled up her arm, taking her by surprise. No wonder the ladies were signing up on his clipboard. She stifled the need to fiddle with her hair.

"Oh, that's fine," she muttered. Then, finding her voice, said, "I'll wait for him to..." Before she could finish her sentence and drop Phil's hand, another man, a few years older but equally attractive with dark hair, appeared at the top of the stairs. Working with such handsome men, after being celibate for over three years, might prove challenging on the composure front. She'd imagined typical stodgy, bespectacled, aging doctors when she'd signed on as a locum. Not a couple of *Gentleman's Quarterly* models.

"That would be Jason," Dr. Hansen said, his smile narrowing his bright blue eyes into crescents. Instead of letting go of her hand, he switched its position and walked her toward the stairs, as if they were old friends. "Here's Stephanie Bennett reporting for duty."

"Great. Come on up, Stephanie. After we talk, I'll show you around."

Phil brought her to the stairway complete with turned spindle rail, dropped her hand on the baluster, and patted it. "Thanks for stepping in," he said in all sincerity. "You'll like it here."

Considering the odd feeling fizzing through her veins, she was inclined to agree.

Stephanie saw the temporary stint in Santa Barbara as the perfect excuse for missing the holidays with her family in Palm Desert. Thanksgiving and Christmas always brought back memories too painful to bear. Not that those thoughts weren't constantly in her mind anyway, but the holidays emphasized *everything*.

The promise of going through the season surrounded by well-meaning loved ones who only managed to make her feel worse was what had driven her to take the new and temporary job. She'd only been dabbling in medicine since the incident that had ripped the life from her heart, shredded her confidence, and caused her marriage to disintegrate. A huge part of her had died that day three years ago.

The Midcoast Medical Clinic of Santa Barbara needed an OB/Gyn doctor for two months. It was the perfect opportunity and timing to get away and maybe, if she was lucky, start to take back her life.

As she walked up the stairs, she overheard Phil. "Okay, I've got one more slot for Friday night."

"I'll take it," the other nurse said, sounding excited.

Was he full of himself? That fizzy feeling evaporated.

Phil sat at his desk, skimming the latest *Pulmonary Physician's Journal* unable to concentrate, wondering what in the hell he was supposed to do with a kid for ten days. But he couldn't turn Roma or his father down.

His father had recently survived his second bout with Hodgkin's lymphoma. His stepmother,

Roma, who was closer to Phil's age than his father's, had called last night. She'd wanted to talk about her plans to take Carl to Maui for some rest and relaxation.

Reasonable enough, right?

No!

Just the two of them, she'd said. Had she lost her powers of reasoning by asking him to care for Robbie? The kid was a dynamo…with special needs.

Robbie, the surprise child for his sixty-five-year-old dad and his fortysomething stepmom, had Down syndrome. The four-year-old, who looked more like a pudgy toddler, always got excited when his "big brother"—make that half brother—came for a visit. Phil didn't mind horsing around with the kid on visits, because he knew he'd go home later on, but taking on his complete care was a whole different thing. Robbie's round face and classic Down syndrome features popped into his mind. The corner of Phil's mouth hitched into a smile. The kid called him Pill. Come on. No fair.

"And it's only for ten days. Your dad needs this trip and if we don't jump on booking it right now we won't get these amazing resort rates and air-fares. Please, please, please!"

Roma knew how to surgically implant the guilt. His father's craggy sun-drenched face, with eyes the color of the ocean, the same eyes Phil had inherited, came to mind. The guy deserved a break.

How could he say no?

Those eyes had lost their sparkle when Phil's mother had left fifteen years ago, the week after he'd first been diagnosed with cancer. How could someone who was supposed to love you do such a thing? Phil had cut his Australian surfing tour short to come home and see his father through the ordeal. It had been a life-changing event for both of them, and he'd never spoken to his mother again. Last he'd heard, she was living in Arizona.

After that, Phil couldn't fathom his dad pulling out of his slump. How could either of them ever trust a woman to stick around?

Carl Hansen had been granted a second chance with Roma, followed by a huge surprise pregnancy. *"Hell, if I wait around for you to settle down and have a grandchild I'll be too old to enjoy it. May as well have my own!"* his father had joked with Phil when he'd first told him the news.

Carl and Roma had had a tough go when Robbie had been diagnosed with Down syndrome after amniocentesis, but they'd wanted him no matter what and hadn't regretted one moment since. Then, after fifteen years of remission, Carl had been hit with cancer again and, on top of being a new parent of a handicapped baby, he'd had to go through chemo. Carl and Roma were nothing less than an inspiration as far as Phil was concerned.

Ten days wasn't a lifetime. Anyone could survive ten days with a kid, right?

"We'll be home in time for Thanksgiving," Roma had said, "and I promise the best meal of your life." Hell, she'd had him at please, please, please.

He'd already started the sign-up sheet for babysitters and backup. Good thing he'd always managed to stay friends with his coworkers and ex-girlfriends—maybe he'd call in a few extra favors.

"You've already met René's replacement, Stephanie Bennett," Jason said, breaking into Phil's thoughts. His partner stood in his office doorway, and beside him the redhead. "She comes with a great endorsement from Eisenhower Medical Center."

All Phil's worries vanished for the time being as he took her in.

Her gaze darted to Jason and back to him, her cheeks flushing pink.

Though noticeably uptight, she had possibilities... Hold it—toddler on board!

"Hi, again. Jason's giving you the official tour, I see." He stood behind his desk. "Let me know if there is ever anything you need, Dr. Bennett."

Her delicate mouth, which sat appealingly beneath an upturned nose, tugged into a tentative smile. "Call me Stephanie," she said, as she tucked the more-red-than-brown, shoulder-length hair behind an ear. "Please."

Though she was saying all the right words, he sensed her standoffishness. He'd never had trouble making friends and acquaintances, especially with women, and sometimes had to remind himself that it didn't come as easy for other people.

"Okay, Stephanie, welcome aboard." He remembered how cool her hand was when he'd shook it, and an old saying came to mind, *Cold hands, warm heart.* It got him thinking about what kind of person she might be behind that cool exterior.

He engaged her sharp gaze, enjoying the little libido kick it gave him. A spark flashed in her butterscotch-colored eyes. Had she felt it too? "Oh, and call me Phil. My extension is 35, same as my age. If you ever need me, I'm right across the hall and I'll be glad to help out."

She nodded her thanks.

"Now let me show you your office," Jason said to Stephanie, ushering her across the waiting room.

As quickly as she'd appeared, she left without looking back. That didn't keep Phil from staring and giving a mental two-note whistle as she followed Jason.

Phil sat and leaned back in his chair, thinking about Stephanie in her copper-and-black patterned jacket, black slacks and the matching stylish lace-lined scoop-neck top. He liked the way her hair was parted on the side and fell in large, loose waves over her cheek and across her shoulders. He liked the set of her jaw, more square than oval yet with a delicate chin. He liked the ivory color of her skin without a hint of the usual freckles of a redhead, and wondered if he might find a few on her nose if he got up close, really close. Just a sprinkling maybe—enough to wipe away that sleek image, enough to make her seem vulnerable beneath her obvious social armor.

And just as he was about to dream a little deeper, his intercom buzzed. It was his nurse. "Your dad's on the phone," she said.

The trip.

Robbie.

How in the hell was he supposed to impress Dr. Bombshell while babysitting his half brother?

Stephanie spent most of the day getting used to the Midcoast Medical OB/Gyn doctor René Munroe's office, as well as the new setup. She'd held a mini-meeting with her nurse, discussing how she liked to run her clinic and telling her exactly what she expected. She wanted to make this transition as smooth as possible, and stuck around later than she'd planned, logged in to the computer, reading patient charts for the next day's appointments. For this stint, she'd concentrate on the gynecological portion of her license.

There had been one stipulation for her taking this job, and Jason Rogers had agreed to it. Though she'd take care of the pregnant patients, she wouldn't be delivering their babies. Fortunately, after perusing the patient files, none of Dr. Munroe's pregnant patients would be at term during her stay. And Jason had eased her concerns by mentioning that it would have been very hard to get her privileges at their local hospital anyway. She'd been in the process of picking up the pieces of her career, knew she could handle the clinical appointment portion, but no way was she ready to deliver a baby again. The thought of holding a tiny bundle of life in her arms sent her nearly over the edge.

Her stomach rumbled and in need of changing her thoughts, she packed up for the day. As she crossed the reception area, the front clinic door swung open and in rushed Phil Hansen with a little dark-haired boy tagging along beside him. The slant of the boy's eyes with epicanthic folds, and the flattened bridge of his nose, hinted at Down syndrome.

"Hold on, Robbie, I've got to make a call," Phil said, shutting off his beeper and reaching over the receptionist's desk to grab the phone.

Robbie smiled at her as only a child with no fear of strangers could. "Hi," he said.

"Hi, there." Her insides tightened and her lungs seemed to forget how to take in air, knowing her son, Justin, would have been close to Robbie's age…if he were still alive. She looked away. Before her eyes could well up, she diverted her thoughts by eavesdropping on Phil's conversation.

"I'll be right there," he said, then hung up and blew out a breath. "Great. What the hell am I supposed to do now?" he mumbled.

She cringed that he cussed so easily around a child.

Phil's gaze found her. A look of desperation made his smooth, handsome features look strained. He glanced at Robbie and back to her. "I need a huge favor. I just got a call from the E.R. One of my patients inhaled his crown while the dentist was replacing it, and I need to do an emergency bronchoscopy to get it out." He dug his fingers into his hair. "Can you watch Robbie for me? I'll only be gone an hour or so."

What? Her, watch a child? "I can't…"

"I don't know what else to do." His blue eyes darkened, wildly darting around the room.

He was obviously in a bind, but didn't he have a child-care provider?

She glanced at the boy, who was oblivious to

Phil's predicament, happily grinning at a picture of a goldfish on the wall.

"Pish!" he said pointing, as if discovering gold.

"I'm really in a bind here," Phil pleaded. "The E.R. is overflowing and they need to get my patient taken care of and discharged. I can't very well plop Robbie down in the E.R. waiting room."

Oh, God, there it was, that lump of maternal instinct she'd pushed out of her mind for the past three years. It planted itself smack in the middle of her chest like an ice pick. She studied Phil, his blue eyes tinted with worry and desperation. She'd give the wrong impression if she refused to help out, and she'd come to Midcoast Medical to help. He'd seemed so sincere earlier when he'd offered his assistance anytime she needed it. A swirl of anxiety twisted her in its clutch as she said, "Okay."

"You'll do it?" He looked stunned, as if he'd just witnessed a miracle.

Well, he had. Never in a million years would

she have volunteered to do this, but as he was in such a bind…

She nodded, and her throat closed up.

"Thank you!" He grabbed her arms and kissed her cheek, releasing her before she had a chance to react. "You're the best."

"What am I supposed to do?"

"Just watch him. I'll be back as soon as I can. Be a good boy for Stephanie, Robbie," he said before he disappeared out the door.

Why couldn't she have left earlier, like everyone else in the clinic? Dread trickled from the crown of her head all the way down to her toes. Her heart knocked against her ribs. She'd made a knee-jerk decision without thinking it through. She couldn't handle this. There went that swirl of panic again, making her knees weak and her hands tremble.

The boy looked at her with innocent eyes, licking his lips. "I'm hungwee."

She couldn't very well ignore the poor kid. "So am I, but I don't have a car seat for you, so we can't go anywhere."

She'd spoken too fast. Obviously, the boy didn't get her point.

He held his tummy and rocked back and forth. "Hungweeeeee."

Oh, God, what should she do now? She scratched her head, aware that a fine line of perspiration had formed above her lip. He was hungry and she was petrified.

Think, Stephanie, think.

She snapped her fingers. The tour. Jason had taken her on a tour of the clinic that morning, and it had included the employee lounge. "Come on, let's check out the refrigerator."

Robbie reached up for her hand. Avoiding his gesture, she quickened her step and started for the hallway. "It's down here," she said, as he toddled behind, bouncing off his toes, trying to catch up.

She switched on lights as they made their way to the kitchen in the mansion-turned-clinic. "Let's see what we can dig up," she said, heading for the refrigerator, avoiding his eyes at all cost and focusing on the task. She had every intention of writing IOU notes for each and everything she found to share with Robbie.

Some impression she'd make on her first day, stealing food.

Heck, the fridge was nearly bare. Someone had trained the employees well about leaving food around to spoil and stink up the place. Fortunately there was a jar of peanut butter. She pulled out drawer after drawer, hoping to find some leftover restaurant-packaged crackers. If the kid got impatient and cried, she'd freak out. Drawer three produced two packs of crackers and a third that was broken into fine pieces. Hopefully, Robbie wouldn't mind crumbs.

"You like peanut butter?"

"Yup," he said, already climbing up on the bench by the table. "I wike milk, too."

Stephanie lifted her brows. "Sorry, can't help you there." But, as all clinics must, they did keep small cartons of juice on hand for their diabetic patients. "Hey, how about some cranberry or orange juice?"

"'Kay."

"Which kind?"

"Boaff."

"Okay. Whatever." Anything to keep the boy busy and happy. Anything to keep him from crying. She glanced at her watch. How long had Phil been gone? Ten minutes? She blew air through her lips. How would she survive an hour?

After their snack, she led him back to the waiting room, careful not to make physical contact, where a small flat-screen TV was wedged in the corner near the ceiling. She didn't have a clue what channels were available in this part of the state, but she needed to keep the boy distracted.

"What do you like to watch?"

"Cartoons!" he said, spinning in a circle of excitement.

She scrolled through the channels and found a cartoon that was nowhere near appropriate for a child.

"That! That!" Robbie called out.

"Uh, that one isn't funny. Let's look for another one." She prayed she could find something that wouldn't shock the boy or teach him bad words. Her hand shook as she continued to flip through the channels. Ah, there it was, just what she'd hoped for, a show with brightly colored puppets with smiling faces and silly voices. Maybe the fist-size knot in her gut would let up now.

She sat on one of the waiting-room chairs, and Robbie invited himself onto her lap. Every muscle in her body stiffened. She couldn't do this. Where was Phil?

His warm little back snuggled against her and when he laughed she could feel it rumble through his chest. She inhaled and smelled the familiar fragrance of children's shampoo, almost bringing her to tears. Someone took good care of this little one. Was it Phil?

She couldn't handle this. Before she jumped out of her skin, she lifted him with outstretched arms and carried him to another chair, closer to the TV.

"Here. This seat is better. You sit here."

Fortunately, engrossed in the show, he didn't

pick up on her tension and sat contentedly staring at the TV.

It had been a long day. She was exhausted, and didn't dare let her guard down. Robbie rubbed his eyes, yawning and soon falling asleep. She paced the waiting room, checked her watch every few seconds, and glanced at the boy as if he were a ticking time bomb. Her throat was so tight, she could barely swallow.

Several minutes passed in this manner. Robbie rested his head on the arm of the chair, sound asleep. Stephanie hoped he'd stay that way until Phil returned.

A few minutes later, one of the puppets on the TV howled, and another joined in. It jolted her. Robbie stirred. His face screwed up. The noise had scared him.

Oh, God, what should she do now?

After a protracted silence, he let out a wail, the kind that used up his breath and left him quiet only long enough to inhale again. Then he let out an even louder wail.

"It's okay, Robbie. It was just the TV," she said

from across the room, trying to console him without getting too close. She patted the air. "It was the show. That's all." She couldn't dare hold him. The thought of holding a child sent lightning bolts of fear through her. She never wanted to do it again.

Flashes of her baby crying, screaming, while she paced the floor, rooted her to the spot. Robbie cried until mucus ran from his nose, and he coughed and sputtered for air, but still she couldn't move.

It took every ounce of strength she had not to bolt out of the clinic.

Phil's patient had been set up and ready for him when he'd arrived in the nearby E.R. The dental crown had been easy to locate in the trachea at the opening of the right bronchus. He'd dislodged it using a rigid scope and forceps, and done a quick check to make sure it hadn't damaged any lung tissue. He'd finished the procedure within ten minutes, leaving the patient to recover with the E.R. nurse.

He barreled through the clinic door, then came to an abrupt stop at the sight of Robbie screaming and Stephanie wild-eyed and pale across the room.

"What's going on?" he said.

She blinked and inhaled, as if coming to life from her statue state. "Thank God, you're back," she whispered.

"What happened?" He rushed to Robbie, picked him up and wiped his nose.

"I was 'cared," Robbie said, starting to cry again.

"Hey, it's okay, buddy, I'm here." Phil hugged his brother as anger overtook him. "What'd you do to him?" he asked, turning as Stephanie ran out the door. What the hell had happened? Confused, he glanced at Robbie. "Did she hurt you?"

"The cartoon monster 'cared me," he whimpered, before crying again.

Phil hugged him, relieved. "Are you hungry, buddy? You want to eat?"

The little guy nodded through his tears. "'Kay," he said with a quiver.

What kind of woman would stand by and let a little kid cry like that? Had she been born without a heart? Phil didn't know what was up with the new doc, but he sure as hell planned to find out first thing tomorrow.

CHAPTER TWO

STEPHANIE snuck in early the next day and lost herself in her patients all morning. She gave a routine physical gynecological examination and ordered labs on the first patient. With her first pregnant client, she measured fundal height and listened to fetal heart tones, discussed nutrition and recommended birthing classes. According to the chart measurements, the third patient's fibroid tumors had actually shrunk in size since her last visit. Stephanie received a high five when she gave the news.

Maybe, if she kept extra-busy, she wouldn't have to confront Phil.

Later, as she performed an initial obstetric examination, she noticed something unusual on the patient's cervix. A plush red and granular-looking area bled easily at her touch. "Have you been having any spotting?"

"No. Is something wrong?" the patient asked.

To be safe, and with concern for the pregnancy, she prepared to take a sample of cells for cytology. "There's a little area on your cervix I want to follow up on. It may be what we call an ectropion, which is an erosion of sorts and is perfectly benign." She left out the part about not wanting to take any chances. "The lab should get results for us within a week."

"What then?"

"If it's negative, which it will most likely be, nothing, unless you have bleeding after sex or if you get frequent infections. Then we'd do something similar to cauterizing it. On the other hand, if the specimen shows abnormal cells, I'll do a biopsy and follow up from there."

"Will it hurt my baby?"

"An ectropion is nothing more than extra vascular tissue. You may have had it a long time, and the pregnancy has changed the shape of your cervix, making it visible."

"But what if you have to do a biopsy?"

How must it feel to have a total stranger deliver such worrisome news? Stephanie inhaled and willed the expertise, professionalism and composure she'd need to help get her through the rest of the appointment. Maybe she shouldn't have said a thing, but what if the test result came back abnormal and she had to drop a bomb? That wouldn't be fair to the patient without a warning. She second-guessed herself and didn't like the repercussions. All the excitement of being pregnant might become overshadowed with fear if she didn't end the appointment on a positive note.

"This small area will most likely just be an irritation. It's quite common. I'm being extra-careful because you're pregnant, and a simple cervical sampling is safe during pregnancy. I'll call with the results as soon as I get them. I promise." She maintained steady eye contact and smiled, then chose a few pamphlets from the wall rack on what to expect when pregnant. "These are filled with great information about your pregnancy. Read them carefully, and afterward, if you have any questions, please feel free to ask me."

The woman's furrowed brow eased just enough for Stephanie to notice. She wanted to hug her and promise everything would be all right, but that was out of her realm as a professional.

"Oh, I almost forgot to tell you your expected due date." She gave the woman the date and saw a huge shift on her face from concern to sheer joy. Her smile felt like a hug, and Stephanie beamed back at her.

"This is a very exciting time, Mrs. Conroy. Enjoy each day," she said, patting the patient's hand.

The young woman accepted the pamphlets, nodded, and prepared to get down from the exam table, her face once again a mixture of expressions. "You'll call as soon as you know anything, right?"

"I promise. You're in great shape, and this pregnancy should go smoothly. A positive attitude is also important."

Stephanie felt like a hypocrite reciting the

words. Her spirits had plunged so low over the past three years she could barely remember what a positive attitude was. If she was going to expect this first-time mother to be upbeat, she should at least try it, too.

After the patient left, she gave herself a little pep talk as she washed her hands. *Just try to have a good time. Do something out of the ordinary. Start living again.*

A figure blocked the exam-room doorway, casting a shadow over the mirror. "You mind telling me what happened last night?" Phil's words were brusque without a hint of yesterday's charm.

Adrenaline surged through her, and she went on the defensive. "I don't do kids." She turned slowly to hide her nerves, and grabbed a paper towel. "You didn't give me a chance to tell you."

"How hard is it to console a crying kid?"

Stephanie held up her hand and looked at Phil's chin rather than into his eyes. "Harder than you could ever understand." She tossed the paper towel into the trash bin and walked around him toward her office. "I'm sorry," she whispered before she closed the door.

Phil scraped his jaw as he walked to his office. What in the hell was her problem? Last night, he'd found her practically huddled in the corner as if in a cage with a lion. It had taken half an hour to console Robbie. A bowl of vanilla ice cream with rainbow sprinkles had finally done the trick. Colorful sprinkles, as Robbie called them. For some dumb reason, Phil got a kick out of that.

What was up with Stephanie Bennett?

He didn't have time to figure out the new doctor when he had more pressing things to do. Like make a schedule! He'd put so much energy into distracting Robbie last night, horsing around with him and watching TV, that he'd lost track of time, forgotten to bathe him and missed his usual bed-time medicine. A kid could survive a day without a bath, right?

His beeper went off. He checked the number. It was the preschool. Hell, what had he forgotten now?

* * *

Stephanie arrived at work extra-early again the next morning, surprised to see someone had already made coffee in the clinic kitchen. She was about to pour herself a cup and sneak back to her office when Phil swept into the room. Her shoulders tensed as she hoped he didn't hold a grudge. Wishing she could disappear, she stayed on task.

"Good morning," he said, looking as if he'd just rolled out of bed, hair left however it had dried after his shower.

"Hi," she said. She didn't want to spend the next two months avoiding one of the clinic partners. Phil had been very nice at first, it seemed to come naturally to him, and, well, she needed him to forgive her. "Look, I'm sorry about the other night."

"Forget about it. Like you said, I didn't leave you much choice." He scrubbed his face as if trying to wake up. "Didn't realize you had a problem with kids." He glanced at her, curiosity in his eyes, but he left all his questions unspoken.

She had no intention of opening up to him, and

hoped he'd let things lie. Maybe if she changed the topic?

She lifted the pot. "Can I pour you a cup, too?"

"Definitely. Robbie kept me up half the night with his coughing."

"Anything wrong?" She leaned against the counter.

"No virus. Just an annoying cough. He's had it since he was a baby." He accepted the proffered mug and took a quick swig. "Ahh."

"So what do you think it is, then?" Discussing medicine was always easy...and safe.

"I've been wondering if he might have tracheo-bronchomalacia, but Roma, his mom, doesn't want him put through a bunch of tests to find out."

"Is that your wife?"

He laughed. "No, my stepmother. Robbie's my half brother."

"Ahh." She'd heard the scuttlebutt about him being quite the playboy, and she couldn't tolerate a married guy flirting with the help.

A smile crossed his face. "Did you think he was my kid?"

She shrugged. What else was she supposed to think?

"I'm just watching Robbie while my dad and Roma are in Maui." He stared at his coffee mug and ran his hand over his hair, deep in thought. "Yeah, so I want to do a bronchoscopy, but Roma is taking some persuading."

"You think like a typical pulmonologist," she said, spooning some sugar into her coffee. "Always the worst-case scenario."

"And you don't assume the worst for your patients?"

She shook her head. "I'm an obstetrician, remember? Good stuff." *Except in her personal life.*

"You've got a point. But I'm not imagining this. He gets recurrent chest infections, he's got a single-note wheeze, and at night he has this constant stridorous cough. I've just never had to sleep with him before."

"You're sleeping with him?" The thought of the

gorgeous guy with the sexy reputation sleeping with his little brother almost brought a smile to her lips.

"Yeah, well…" Did Phil look sheepish? "He was in a new house and a strange bed. You know the drill."

She couldn't hide her smile any longer. "That's very sweet."

He cleared his throat and stood a little straighter, a more macho pose. "More like survival. The kid cried until I promised to sleep with him."

Heat worked up her neck. "That was probably my fault."

He looked at her, and their eyes met for the briefest of moments. There was a real human being behind that ruggedly handsome face. Perhaps someone worth knowing.

"Let's drop it. As far as I'm concerned, it never happened," he said.

Maybe she shouldn't try so hard to avoid him. Maybe he was a great guy she could enjoy. But insecurity, like well-worn shoes you just couldn't part with, kept her from giving him a second thought.

"It's not asthma," he said, breaking her concentration. "If I knew for sure what it was, I could treat it. He may grow out of it, but he's suffering right now. You think I look tired, you should see him. The thing is, he might only need something as simple as extra oxygen or, if necessary, CPAP." He rubbed his chin.

All the talk about Robbie's respiratory condition made her worry about him. Especially after she'd made the poor little guy cry until he was hoarse the other night. She sipped her coffee. "Is there any less invasive procedure that can give the same diagnosis?" Keeping things technical made it easier to talk about the boy.

"Bronchography, but he's allergic to iodine, and I wouldn't want to expose him to the radiation at this age. And all I'd have to do is sedate him and slip a scope in his lungs to check things out. Five minutes, tops. I'll see how things go."

"So where is he?"

"He's in day care with his new best friend,

Claire's daughter. Thankfully she took pity on me and chauffeured him today."

No sooner had he said it than Claire breezed through the door. The tall, slender, honey blonde had a mischievous glint in her eyes. "It's called carpooling."

"Ah, right." Phil said, then glanced at Stephanie. "Learning curve."

"Morning," Claire said.

Stephanie nodded. She'd met the clinic nurse practitioner the other day in a bright, welcoming office that came complete with aromatherapy and candles. She was Jason's wife, and seemed nice enough, but Stephanie hadn't let herself warm to anyone yet.

"So, Robbie didn't want to go with his group after driving to the preschool with Gina talking his ear off," Claire said. "Gina's my daughter," she said for Stephanie's benefit. "He looks so cute in his glasses. When did he get them?"

Phil grinned. "Beats me, but I found them in his things, so I talked him into wearing them."

"See, you're a natural."

He refilled half of his mug. "That'll be the day. Two nights, and I'm already planning to scope him for that cough of his. How does Roma manage?"

"Like all mothers. We follow our instincts. Give it a try." Claire winked at Stephanie, as if they belonged to the same secret sorority. If Claire only knew how wrong she was.

Stephanie took another swallow of coffee, wishing she could fade into the woodwork.

"Do you have any kids?" Claire asked.

"No." Stephanie couldn't say it fast enough. She stared deeply into her coffee, trying her best to compose herself. Phil watched her. "Well, I'd better prepare for my first patient. I have a lot to live up to, filling René's shoes." She reheated her coffee and started for the door, needing to get far away from all the talk of children. Maybe it had been a mistake coming here, but she'd committed herself for the next two months, and she'd live up to her promise.

"You'll do fine," Phil said with a reassuring

smile. "I've got to take off, too. Need to make a run to the hospital this morning."

She peeked over her shoulder. He stopped and poured the rest of his coffee into the sink, then glanced at Stephanie. Eye contact with Phil was the last thing she wanted, so she flicked her gaze toward her shoes. What must he think of her and her crazy behavior? But, more importantly, why did she care?

On her way out the door she passed the cardiologist, Jon Becker, and nodded. He gave a stately nod then headed for the counter and the nearly empty coffee pot.

"Hey," he said. "I made the coffee and now all I get is half a cup?"

Hunching her shoulders, Stephanie took a surreptitious sip from her mug and slunk down the hall. How many more bad first impressions was she going to make?

"Make a full pot next time," she heard Claire say. "Quit being so task oriented," she chided, more as if to a family member than a business colleague. "If you're going to be a stay-at-home dad, you need to think like a nurturer."

"Claire, all I wanted was a cup of coffee, not a feminist lecture on thinking for the group."

Stephanie couldn't resist it. A smile stretched across her lips, the first one in two days. Jon looked at least forty, and he was going to be a stay-at-home dad?

She'd been so isolated over the past three years, and had no idea how to have a simple conversation with coworkers. Maybe it was time to make an effort to be friendly, like every other normal human being.

A familiar negative tidal wave moved swiftly and blanketed her with doubt.

You don't deserve to be alive. She could practically hear her ex-husband's voice repeating the cutting words.

On her way back to the extended-stay hotel that night, Stephanie realized how famished she was. On a whim, she stopped at a decent-looking Japanese restaurant for some takeout.

After placing her order, she sat primly on the edge of one of the sushi bar stools. She sipped green tea, and glanced around. Down the aisle, there was Robbie, grains of rice stuck to his beaming face like 3-D freckles. Across from the boy, with his back to her, sat Phil. A jolt of nerves cut through her as she hoped Robbie wouldn't recognize her. He might start crying again. How soon could she get her order and sneak out? Just as she thought it, as if sending a mental tap to his shoulder, Phil turned and saw her, flashed a look of surprise, then waved her over.

She couldn't very well pretend she hadn't seen him. She waved tentatively back then shook her head as Phil's ever-broadening gesture to join them was accompanied by a desperate look.

Be strong. He's the one babysitting. It's not your responsibility.

He stood, made an even more pronounced gesture with pleading eyes.

The guy begged, but she couldn't budge. She shook her head and mouthed, "Sorry." He might think she was the most unfriendly woman he'd ever met, but no way was she ready to sit down with them, as if they were some little happy family. No. She couldn't. It would be unbearable.

She avoided Phil's disappointed gaze by finishing her tea.

Fortunately, the sushi chef handed her the order. After she paid for the food, she grabbed the package, tossed Phil one last regretful look, and left.

Strike two.

Stephanie walked her last patient of the morning to the door. The lady hugged her as if they were old friends. One of the things she loved about her job was telling people they were pregnant.

"Have you got all the information you need?"

The young woman's head bobbed.

"Any more questions?"

"I'm sure I've got a million of them, but I can't think of anything right now except…I'm pregnant!" She clapped her hands.

Stephanie laughed. "Well, be sure to write all those questions down and we'll go through them next time."

"I will, Doctor. Thanks again." The woman gave her a second hug.

Stephanie waved goodbye, and with a smile on her face watched as her patient floated on air when she left the clinic.

"I was about to accuse you of being heartless, but I've changed my mind now," Phil chided.

Stephanie blushed. She knew exactly what he referred to.

"How are things going with Robbie?" her nurse asked Phil in passing.

"Just dandy," he said, with a wry smile. "I finally figured out it's a lot less messy to take him into the shower with me instead of bathing him in the tub by himself."

The nurse giggled. "I can only imagine."

Stephanie fought the image his description implanted in her mind, obviously the same one Amy had. He seemed to be a nice guy. Everyone liked him. Adored him. The fact that he was billboard gorgeous, even with ever-darkening circles under his eyes, should be a plus, but it intimidated her. And after the way she'd treated him and Robbie, she didn't have a clue why he kept coming around.

"You doing anything for lunch today?" he asked.

Could she handle an entire lunch with this guy? "Why would you want to take me to lunch?"

"Why not? You're new in town, probably don't know your way around…"

His cell phone went off, saving her from answering him.

"Cripes!" he said. "Hold on a sec." He held up one finger and answered his phone.

After a brief conversation, he hung up with a dejected look. "Evidently Robbie got pushed by another kid and skinned his knees." He scratched his head, a look of bewilderment in his eyes. "He's crying and asking for me, so…"

"It's a big job being a stand-in dad, isn't it?"

"You're telling me. Hey, I have an idea, why don't we have lunch tomorrow?"

Swept up by the whole package that was Phil, including the part of fumbling stand-in dad, she answered without thinking. "Sure."

* * *

The next day, at noon, Stephanie found Phil standing at her door wearing another expression of chagrin. "I completely forgot we have a staff meeting today."

"Yeah, I just got the memo," she said.

"You should come. We've got some big decisions to make."

"I don't have any authority here."

"Oh, trust me, on this topic your input is equally as important as any of ours."

"What are you talking about?"

"We have to decide how we're going to decorate the yacht for the annual Christmas parade."

"It's not even Thanksgiving yet!"

"Big ideas take big planning. Besides, have you been by the Paseo? They've already put up a Christmas tree. Huge thing, too. I took Robbie to see it last night."

His deadpan expression and quirky news made her blurt a laugh. When was the last time she'd done that? "Well, seeing I've never been on a yacht, not to mention the fact that I suck at decorating, I can't see how I'll bring a lot to the table."

"Come anyway. You might enjoy it."

I might enjoy it. Wasn't that the pep talk she'd given herself the other day? Be open to new things? Start acting alive again?

"It's a free lunch," he enticed with lowered sun-bleached brows.

"I'll think about it."

"If you change your mind, we'll be in the lounge in ten minutes."

"Okay."

His smile started at those shocking blue eyes, traveled down to his enticing mouth and wound up looking suspiciously like victory. The guy was one smooth operator.

After he left, Stephanie surprised herself further when she brushed her hair, plumped and puffed it into submission, then put on a new coat of lip gloss before heading to the back of the building for the meeting. She stopped at the double doors, fighting back the nervous wave waiting to pounce. The place was abuzz with activity. Claire called out various types of sandwiches she had stored in a huge shopping bag, and when someone claimed one, she tossed the securely wrapped package at them. One of the nurses passed out canned sodas or bottled water. Another gave a choice of fruit or cookie.

"I'll take both," she heard Phil say just before he noticed her at the door. "Hey, I saved you a seat." He patted the chair next to him. "What kind of sandwich do you want?"

"Turkey?"

"We need a turkey over here," he called to Claire.

Stephanie ducked as the lunch missile almost hit her head before she could sit. A smile worked its way from one side of her mouth to the other. These people might be crazy, but they were fun.

"Sorry!" Claire called out.

"No problem." She had to admit that she kind of liked this friendly chaos. It was distracting, and that was always a good thing. When her gaze settled on Phil, he was already watching her, a smile very similar to the one she'd seen in her office lingering on his lips.

"I'm glad you decided to come."

If he was a player, she got the distinct impression he was circling her. How in the world should she feel about that? Lunch was one thing, but what if he asked her out? Hearing how he struggled with Robbie had shown her another side of him. This guy had a heart beneath all that puffed-up male plumage, she'd bet her first paycheck on it. She wasn't sure she could make the same claim for herself.

"Okay, everybody, let's get going on this." Jason stood at the head of the long table, his mere presence commanding attention. Dark hair, pewter eyes, suntanned face, she could see why Claire watched him so adoringly. "Last year we came in third in the Santa Barbara Chamber of Commerce Christmas Ocean Parade, and this year I think we have a fighting chance of taking first if we put our heads together and come up with a theme."

"You mean like Christmas at Christmastime?" Jon looked perplexed by the obvious.

"He means like Santa and his helpers, or

Christmas shopping mania, or the North Pole," Claire shot back.

"How about trains?" Jon said. "Boys love trains at Christmas."

"What about trains and dolls?" Jon's nurse added, with a wayward glance.

"How about Christmas around the world?" Stephanie's nurse, Amy, spoke up. "We could cover the yacht with small Christmas trees decorated the way other countries do, and the mast could be a huge Christmas tree all made from lights."

The conversation buzzed and hummed in response to the first ideas. It seemed everyone had a suggestion. Everyone but Stephanie. She particularly liked what Amy had suggested.

What did she remember most from Christmas besides the beautifully decorated trees? Santa, that's what. "Could we have a Santa by the big tree?" She said her thought out loud by mistake.

"Yeah, we need a Santa up there," Phil backed her up.

"And I nominate you to be Santa," Claire said, pointing to Phil with an impish smile. "You'd be adorable."

"Me! You've got to be kidding! I scare kids."

"Oh, right, and Robbie doesn't adore you. Yeah, I think you should be Santa and Gina and Robbie can sit on your lap." Claire wouldn't back down.

"No way," he said, with an *are-you-crazy* glare in his eyes. Out of the corner of his mouth he said, "Thanks a lot," to Stephanie.

"Great idea," one of the nurses blurted across the table, before a few others chimed in. "Yeah."

"But I am the *un*-Santa." He glanced at Stephanie again, this time with a back-me-up-here plea in his eyes.

Not about to get involved in the debate, she lifted her brows, shrugged and took a bite of her sandwich.

"Look," Jason said. "We need to get more people involved on the yacht, and you haven't been much help the last couple of years." There was a sparkle in Jason's eyes, as if he enjoyed putting Phil on the spot. "Should everyone be elves?" he asked, his mouth half-full of sandwich.

"What if one person stood by each decorated country's tree dressed in the traditional outfit?" Amy seemed to be on a roll. "You know, lederhosen, kilt, cowboy hat…oh, and what's that Russian fur thing called? Ushanka? And what about a dashiki or caftan, oh, wait, and a kimono, or a sari or…"

"That's a fantastic idea," Claire said.

Revved up, Amy grinned, and Stephanie nodded with approval at her. Phil squeezed her forearm. Okay, everything was a great idea except for Santa.

General agreement hummed through the room, and several people soon chimed in. *Wow. I like that. Good idea.*

The receptionist, Gaby, wearing glasses that covered half of her face, took notes like a court reporter.

"Did you get that?" Jason asked her.

Gaby nodded, never looking up, not breaking her bound-for-writer's-cramp speed.

"Ah, then we shouldn't need a Santa anymore," Phil said, sounding relieved.

"Of course we will," Claire said. "One Santa unites them all, and Phil will be it."

Stephanie's eyes widened and from the side, she noticed his narrow betrayed-looking gaze directed at Claire.

"I say we take a vote on who should be Santa, the captain of the boat or me," he said, just before his beeper went off. "Damn. It's day care. I've got to take this." He strode out of the room, the doors swinging in his wake.

Jason snagged the opportunity. "Okay, everyone agree Phil's Santa?"

Everyone laughed and nodded. Poor guy didn't stand a chance. Stephanie had to admit she sort of felt sorry for him.

Phil stepped back into the room, half of his mouth hitched but not in a smile. "I've got to make a quick run over to day care. Robbie's refusing to cooperate with nap time."

Jason nodded. "Let us know if you need to reschedule some appointments."

"It shouldn't take long. I've just got to make the kid understand he has to follow the rules—" Phil snapped his fingers as if the greatest idea in the universe had just occurred to him "—or he won't get afternoon snack!"

Stephanie laughed. The guy was barely coping with this new responsibility, but he wasn't griping. He seemed to catch on quickly, and, she had to admit, it made her like him even more. She glanced around the table at all the adoring female gazes on him. Okay, so she'd finally joined the club.

"So who's Santa this year?" Phil asked, one hand on the door.

Jason grinned. "You!"

He flashed a glance at Stephanie, pointed, and mouthed, "You owe me."

CHAPTER THREE

PHIL finished entering the list of orders in the computer for his last patient of the afternoon. His mind had been wandering between the appointments, and Stephanie Bennett was the reason. She was as guarded as a locked box. Then out of nowhere today this fun-loving Santa-of-the-world fan had emerged, and it had backfired and landed him on a date with a red suit.

Something held her back from enjoying life, and he'd probably never find out in two months what it was, but romantic that he was, he still wanted to get to know her better. The time restraint was a perfect excuse to keep things casual and uninvolved. Just his style.

But there was Robbie—a full-time job. No way could he squeeze in a romantic fling until his father and Roma came home.

He pushed Enter on the computer program and shut it down.

Good thing he'd lined up Gaby for child care on Saturday morning.

Jason had asked him to stop by his office on his way out today, so he trotted up the back stairs to the second floor. Aw, damn, he'd caught Jason and Claire kissing. He stepped back from the doorway. They seemed to do that a lot and hadn't even heard him. Yeah, they were newlyweds but, still, they were married, with children! He marveled at the phenomenon. Come to think of it, his dad and Roma did a lot of smooching, too.

Maybe players like him didn't corner the market on romance.

He decided to talk to Jason later, then padded down the stairs and veered toward Stephanie's office, a place he'd been drawn to like a magnet lately. Just as he passed Jon's door he heard his name.

"Hey, Phil, come take a look at the latest pictures."

Oh, man, he knew exactly what those pictures

would be. Evan, his newborn son, seemed to be the center of Jon's universe these days. Being just outside Jon's office, Phil couldn't very well avoid the invitation.

What was with his partners? They'd all settled down, leaving him the lone bachelor. The thing that really perplexed him was that they all seemed so damn blissful. Well, he wasn't into matrimonial bliss. No way. No how. He liked his freedom. Liked being alone. He glanced at Stephanie's office. At least now he knew someone else who liked being single.

Except for Robbie staying with him, he hadn't lived with anyone since his med-school roommates. And he really didn't miss their stinky socks and dirty underwear tossed around the cramped apartment. Come to think of it, Robbie's socks ran a close second, and the kid knew nothing about putting things away. He smiled at the image of his little half brother strutting around in his underwear with pictures of superheroes pasted all over. Even his nighttime diapers had cartoon characters decorating them. What in the world had his life turned into?

An odd sensation tugged somewhere so buried inside he couldn't locate it, but the feeling still managed to get his attention. *Heads up, dude. Take note. Maybe there's something to be said for a good relationship and a family.*

No. Way. Maybe it worked for other people, but he wasn't capable of sustaining a long-term love affair. Wasn't interested. He knew just as many people whose marriages didn't work out. Hell, his own mother had walked out on them.

Nope. He liked the here and now, and when things got too deep or involved, he was out of there. Maybe he was more like his mom than he wanted to admit. His list of ex-girlfriends kept growing; many of them had since married and he was glad for them. It just wasn't his thing.

Phil greeted Jon and fulfilled his obligation as a good coworker to ooh and aah over Jon and René's new son. Then he patted him on the back, told him he was a lucky dog, and excused himself with a perfectly valid reason. "I've got to pick up Robbie."

On his way out of the clinic, he glanced at Stephanie's closed office door. What were the odds of him running into her at dinner again tonight?

Nope. If he wanted to spend some more time with her, he couldn't depend on something as flimsy as fate. He'd need a plan.

Gaby had signed up to watch Robbie on Saturday morning. Maybe he'd make plans with Stephanie then. As for dinner tonight, he had a date with his kid brother for a grilled cheese sandwich and tomato soup.

Just seven more days.

Stephanie was aware that René mentored nurse practitioner students from the local university once a week, but hadn't realized she'd be taking on this aspect of René's job along with everything else. Thursday morning she was shadowed by a bright and pregnant-as-she-was-tall young woman filled with questions. Maria Avila had thick black hair and wore it piled on top of her head, and if she was trying to look taller, the extra hair didn't help. Her shining dark eyes oozed intelligence and curiosity and her pleasant personality suited Stephanie just fine. After a full morning together, they prepared for the last appointment.

"If my next patient consents, I'll guide you through bimanual pelvic examination."

Stephanie fought back a laugh at the student's excitement when she pumped the air with her fist.

"Have you done one before?"

"I've done them in class with a human-looking model," Maria said.

Stephanie raised her brows. "That's not nearly the same thing. I'll do my best to get this opportunity for you. Now, here's the woman's story." Stephanie recited the medical history from the computer for Maria. "What would you do for her today?"

Maria sat pensively for a few minutes then ran down a list of questions she'd ask and labs she'd recommend. Her instincts were right-on, and

Stephanie thought she'd make a good care provider one day.

The examination went well, Stephanie stepped in to collect the Pap smear, and Maria was ecstatic she got hands-on experience. Fortunately the patient was fine with the extra medical care as long as Stephanie followed up with her own examination.

One of the ovaries was larger than normal, and tender to the touch. It could be something as simple as a cyst, but she wanted to make sure. She also wanted Maria to feel the small, subtle mass that she'd overlooked when she'd first performed the exam.

From the woman's history she knew there wasn't any ovarian cancer in her immediate family. She met some of the other risk factors, though. She had never been pregnant, was over fifty-five, and postmenopausal.

"Have you had any pain or pressure in your abdomen lately?"

The woman shook her head.

"Bloating or indigestion?"

"Doesn't every woman get that?" the patient said, with a wry smile.

"You've got a point there." Stephanie grinned back.

When she finished the exam, as she removed the gloves and washed her hands, she mentioned her plan of action. "I'm ordering a pelvic ultrasound to rule out a small cyst." She didn't want to alarm the woman about the potential for cancer due to her age, but finding any pathology early was the name of the game when it came to that disease. "I'll request the study ASAP."

The grateful woman thanked both of them and on her way out she hugged the student RNP, Maria. "Good luck with your pregnancy, and keep up your training. We need more people in the field."

Her comment drove Stephanie to ask, "Are you in medicine?"

"I'm a nurse."

Stephanie figured, being a nurse, the patient was already in a panic about what her slightly enlarged ovary might be.

"Don't drive yourself crazy worrying about the worst-case scenario, Ms. Winkler, okay? The nodule didn't feel hard or immovable. It's most likely a cyst."

The extra reassurance helped smooth the woman's wrinkled brow, but nervous tension was still evident in her eyes when she left.

Stephanie briefed Maria on possible reasons why she'd missed the subtle change in the ovary and offered suggestions on hand placement while performing future examinations for best results.

They walked back to her office as Stephanie explained further for Maria.

"The worst thing we can do is leave a patient waiting for results, but sometimes our job is like a guessing game. We have to go through each step to rule out the problem. Fortunately, modern medicine usually gives us great results in a timely manner."

"Waxing philosophical, Doc?" Phil's distinct voice sent a quick chill down her spine.

How long had it been since that had happened with a man? Not since the first morning when she'd seen him, to be exact. "Can I do something for you, Phil?"

With a slow smile, he glanced first at Stephanie then at Maria, whose cheeks blushed almost immediately. What was with his power over women?

"Yeah. You can meet me at Stearn's Wharf Saturday morning around nine."

Was this his idea of asking her out? In front of the student nurse practitioner?

"Uh. You sort of caught me off guard."

"Hmm. Like how you bamboozled me into being Santa?"

Okay, now she got it. It was payback time. She grimaced. "If it matters at all, I abstained from voting."

"Warms my heart, Doc." He patted his chest over his white doctor's coat.

But meeting at the beach for what was predicted to be yet another gorgeous Santa Barbara day sounded more like reward than payback.

Maria cleared her throat. "I should be going and let you two work this out."

"Oh, right." Stephanie felt a blush begin. What kind of impression would she make with her student, making plans for a date right in front of her?

"Thanks so much, Dr. Bennett. You've been fantastic and I've learned a lot today," Maria said.

"You're welcome, and I guess I'll see you next week?"

"Actually, that's Thanksgiving. But I'll be here the week after, that is if I don't go into premature labor first!" The otherwise elfin woman beamed a smile, looked at Dr. Hansen again, subtly turned so only Stephanie could see her face, and mouthed, "Wow!" with crossed eyes to emphasize his affect on her, then left.

Stephanie didn't even try to hide her grin. *Yeah, he's hunky.*

Stephanie couldn't have asked for a more beautiful day on Saturday morning. There wasn't a cloud in the cornflower-blue sky, and the sun spread its warmth on the top of her head and shoulders, making the brisk temperature refreshing. The ocean, like glittering blue glass along the horizon, tossed and rolled against the pier pilings, as raucous seagulls circled overhead. At home, the clean desert air was dry and gritty, but here on the wharf the ocean breeze with its briny scent energized her.

She hadn't exactly said yes or no to Phil's proposition on Thursday. She'd said she'd think about it, and he'd said he was planning to surf that morning anyway, so come if she felt like it. Well, she'd felt like it, and by virtue of the glorious view, she was already glad about her decision.

A group of surfers was a few hundred yards to the left of the pier, and though the odds were stacked against her, she tried to pick out Phil. With everyone wearing wet suits, it proved to be an impossible task.

"Here's some coffee."

Jumping, Stephanie pivoted to find Phil decked out in a wet suit, holding his surfboard under one arm and a take-out cup of coffee in another.

He handed it to her as she worked at closing her mouth.

He was a vision in black neoprene. The suit left nothing of his sculpted body to her imagination—from neck to shoulders to thighs to calves, every part of him was pure perfection.

"Thanks," she said, taking the coffee, unable to think of a single thing to say.

"I'm glad you showed up."

"Me, too."

"If you're still around later, I'll meet you on the beach in…" he glanced at a waterproof watch "…say an hour or so," he said, throwing his board over the forty-foot-high rail.

She watched in horror as he hopped onto the wood post and dived into the ocean. Was he crazy?

"Hey, no jumping from the pier!" a gruff voice yelled from behind. The white-haired security guard didn't stand a chance of catching him.

Stephanie gulped and looked over the rail just as Phil surfaced. He swam to his board, straddled it like a horse, looked up and waved. *Yee haw!*

She shook her head, waiting for the surge of adrenaline to wane. "You almost gave me a heart attack," she yelled.

He laughed. "This is the lazy man's way of getting past the breakers," he shouted with a huge grin. "Enjoy your coffee. I'll see you on the beach later."

He paddled off, and like an expert he caught the first wave, dipping through the curl, zigzagging, riding it until it lost its momentum.

As she sipped her coffee, she watched Phil surf wave after wave, never faltering. He looked like Adonis in a wet suit playing among the mere humans. Today the ocean was only moderately roiled up, offering him little challenge and nothing he couldn't handle standing on one leg. But it was still exciting to see him in action. She remembered several pictures on his office wall with his surfboard planted in the sand like a fat and oddly shaped palm tree, and him receiving a trophy from someone, or a kiss from an equally gorgeous girl. What a charmed life he must lead. Doctor by day, surfer by weekend.

She checked her watch after an hour or so and began walking back to the mouth of the pier. After removing her shoes, she strolled along the wet, gritty sand as she watched Phil ride the curl of a strong, high wave almost all the way to the shore.

He stepped off his board as if off a magic carpet, bent to tuck it under his arm, and waded the remaining distance to where she stood.

"You make it look so easy," she said, waving and smiling.

"I've been surfing since I was twelve."

All man—hair slicked back from his face curling just below his ears, sea water dripping down his temples, broad shoulders and narrow hips—the last thing she could envision was Phil as a prepubescent boy.

"Second nature, huh?"

"Something like that. Hey, I know a great little stand that sells the best hot dogs in Santa Barbara. If you like chili dogs, I'll get out of this suit and we can walk over there."

She nodded as he pointed to the street and the

amazingly lucky parking place he'd managed to snag. They walked in friendly conversation toward his car, a classic 1950s Woodie, the signature surfer wagon, complete with side wood paneling.

"Oh, my gosh, this is fantastic!" she said.

"My dad gave me this for my sixteenth birthday, when he realized surfing was my passion."

"It's gorgeous." *So are you.*

For the first time that day, Phil made an obvious head-to-toe assessment of Stephanie. She'd worn shorts, a tank top and zipped hoodie sweatshirt. "You're looking pretty damn great yourself."

A self-conscious thought about her pale legs, compared to his golden-bronze skin, made her wish she'd worn her tried-and-trusted jeans, but seeing the pleased look on his face as he stared at her changed her mind.

He unzipped his wet suit and peeled it off his arms and down to his waist, revealing a flat stomach, cut torso, and defined chest. Just as Stephanie began to worry about what a guy wore under a wet suit, he tugged down the garment to reveal black trunks.

Oh, my. Seeing so much of Phil Hansen was making her mouth water.

He threw a pair of cargo shorts over the trunks, ducked his head into a T-shirt, and in record time slid into some well-worn leather flip-flops.

"You ready?" he said, shaking out his hair.

"Sure," she said, completely under his wet-and-wild spell.

"Oh, hey, wait," he said, closing and locking the hatch. "I forgot something." He took a step toward her, pulled her close, and kissed her.

His mouth was warm and soft as it covered her lips ever so gently. They were nearly strangers, and this wasn't how she did things, but she couldn't manage to tear herself away. Shock made her edgy...at first. The kiss, like a calming tide, swept over her head to toe, smoothing and relaxing her resistance. She wanted more and pressed into his welcoming lips.

When his hands went to her waist, she tensed again. Their heat started a mini-implosion over her hips, sending pleasant waves throughout her body. She wasn't ready to touch him back, except for right there on those inviting lips. She inhaled the scent of ocean on his skin, and breathed deeper, tasting sea salt as she flicked the smooth lining of his mouth with her tongue.

Their connection seemed to stop time. Her hands dangled at her sides, more out of concern about where it might lead if she touched his broad shoulders. Though she wanted to. She wanted to explore every part of Phil Hansen, but they were in public on a busy street. This was no time or place for a first kiss of this magnitude.

Still, she didn't move, kept kissing him, savored the sweet, tender, first kiss. A basic, female re-action flowed through her core, warming every-thing in its path from the tips of her breasts down to the ends of her toes. She hadn't felt this kind of heady response since she'd first fallen in love with her husband.

Her ex-husband.

Okay, that put the hex on this kiss. Aside from the fact that Phil was a good kisser—restrained, not mauling; gentle, not immediately going for the touchdown—and aside from the fact that she liked how he felt—really liked how he kissed— the thought of her condemning and unforgiving ex ruined the moment.

She broke contact and pulled back. He studied her up close as if reading her mind. He wasn't rude or persistent. He knew they'd had their moment and now it was over, yet his probing stare let her know he understood something was up, and that he'd respect whatever the barrier was…for now.

What she saw in the depths of his eyes unsettled her. Besides everything his kiss had done, from heating her up inside to sending chills over her skin, she could read in his look that it was only a matter of time before they'd be doing this kissing business again.

The unspoken promise both thrilled and scared her.

CHAPTER FOUR

PHIL had promised a world-class hot dog and he hadn't let Stephanie down. They sat at a little metal table on the cement walk in front of a red-and-white striped awning on Cabrillo Boulevard. Still trying her best to recover from Phil's kiss, she concentrated on eating the dog slathered in heart-clogging chili topped with cheese, and not the imposingly appealing man across the table... staring at her.

"You said you started surfing at twelve?" she said.

She could handle lunch with Phil. If she repeated it enough times maybe she'd believe it. Tell that to her pulse, which quickened every time she noticed new things about him, like how his sideburns were perfectly matched and at least three shades darker than his hair, with a tinge of red.

Just before she took her first bite of hot dog, she wondered what his beard stubble might feel like first thing in the morning, and almost missed her mouth.

"Yeah. I had a knack." He smiled at her and her heart stepped out of rhythm. He had a "knack" for world-class kisses, too. "I was spoiled and my parents let me do just about everything. By the time I was fourteen, I got recruited for the Corona Pro surf circuit, and the rest…" he delivered another one of his knockout smiles "…as they say, is history."

"Growing up in the desert, surfing wasn't exactly on my list of things to do. I'm more of a volleyball girl myself."

He raised one brow with interest. "Ever played beach volleyball?"

She shook her head and reached for her soda. "Looks too grueling with all that sand."

"They play beach volleyball every weekend right down the street." He pointed behind him with his thumb.

"Oh, yeah, I remember I saw the nets the day I drove into town."

"So what do you say? Want to check out the game tomorrow?"

"What about Robbie?"

He sat straighter. "I'll bring him along."

She gave him a hesitant glance; her throat tightened, making it hard to swallow the tastiest chili she'd ever eaten.

"You see right through me, don't you?" he said. "Truth is, I need some help keeping the kid entertained, and I've already run out of ideas."

"Well, don't look at me," she said, swallowing and taking another bite.

His playful gaze grew serious. "What's the deal? I mean, I've never seen…"

Should she tell him? By all accounts, he was still a stranger…who'd kissed her senseless. Did he deserve to know her deepest secret just because he was curious?

"The thing is…" Two years ago she'd had her tubes tied to cement the point. "I don't do kids." No. Better to keep it vague. Keep the distance.

"But you deliver babies for a living," Phil said, arms crossed over his black T-shirt, brows furrowed, obviously confused.

"I deliver *other people's* babies." She took another bite of her hot dog and did her best to pretend there wasn't anything contradictory about the statement.

Phil finished his first hot dog, washed it down with cola and wiped his mouth. Stephanie intrigued him with this inconsistency—an OB doc who didn't do babies. And she was quickly becoming his dream date. When a woman didn't want kids, marriage didn't seem to be a priority. And since marriage was the last thing on his to-do list, maybe they could have a good time together, for however long this attraction lasted.

Beneath her defiant remark "I don't do babies" he noticed one telling sign—hurt. He could see it in her gaze. Those inviting butterscotch-with-flecks-of-gold eyes went dull at the mention of kids. Something had caused her great pain and the result made her avoid children. He flashed to the moment he'd walked into the clinic the first night, how he'd seen terror in her expression, how she hadn't been able to get away fast enough. He needed to play this cool, or she'd bolt again.

"No wonder you looked so uncomfortable when I left Robbie with you." He wiped mustard from the corner of his mouth.

She gave a wry laugh as a quick blush pinkened her cheeks. "Uncomfortable is a generous description."

"Yeah, okay, more like you freaked out."

She nodded. "Sorry."

"It's all right."

She made a half-hearted attempt at a smile, and his heart went out to her. He needed to lighten the mood. Maybe he could tease her into submission.

"So there's no chance I can change your mind?" He put his hand on top of hers, immediately aware of how fragile she felt.

"Maybe some other time."

"Translation being—get lost, Phil?"

"Not at all." She met his gaze, sending a subtle message, then quickly looked away.

So maybe she was interested in him, just not the whole Phil-and-Robbie package. Once he sent Robbie back to his stepmom and dad, he'd have time to enjoy her company up close and, hopefully, very personal. Especially after that kiss confirmed what he'd suspected since the first day he'd seen her—they had chemistry. And knowing she didn't want to get involved with anyone any more than he did sounded like the perfect setup.

"Okay. I get it. But when my parents get back from Hawaii, and Robbie goes home, I'd like to make an official date with you."

He hadn't removed his hand, and hers turned beneath his. Now palm to palm, a stimulating image formed in his mind. He wished he could take her home and ravish her right on the spot, but she was skittish and he needed to take things slowly.

"Fine." She flicked her lashes and glanced quickly into his eyes, then slid her hand away.

Still high from their kiss, new desire stirred in him. From the jolt he felt, she could have been throwing lightning bolts instead of batting her lashes. They definitely had chemistry.

"Fine?" he said. "Well, then, let's make that date right now, so I'll have something to look forward to."

On Saturday night, Phil watched Robbie sleep. The little guy flipped and flopped and in between he coughed. His eyes popped open for the briefest of moments, fluttered, then clamped shut as if trying desperately to stay asleep, but the constant irritation of that cough gave him a good battle. The restless spectacle put a hard lump smack in the middle of Phil's throat.

Robbie's world would become difficult enough as he got older and realized that other kids looked at him differently, and maybe they wouldn't play with him because of him having Down syndrome.

"Sweet kid," he mumbled against an alien yet firm tugging in his chest. What was happening to him?

He adjusted the covers for the umpteenth time

beneath his little brother's chin before taking a stroll to the kitchen for a glass of water. It had taken a few days, but they were starting to get into a routine at night. Robbie had filled him in on the rule about reading a picture book before bed. Phil had complied. Heck, he even enjoyed some of them. After a couple of nights, Phil was even able to sneak back to his own bed.

Robbie drifted in a sweet oblivious tide of ignorance and bliss hanging out with other toddlers. How much longer would it last? And as long as it did last, Phil wanted nothing more than for him to be well rested and on his best play-pal game at preschool.

When Robbie didn't sleep, Phil didn't either. How in hell had Roma and his dad managed the last four years?

And when Phil couldn't sleep, his mind drifted to Stephanie—the last person he needed to think about if he had any hope of getting rest. Maybe he'd taken advantage of the situation by kissing her at the beach, even though she'd done her share of participation with that kiss. It had been a whim.

She'd looked so damn sweet and vulnerable, completely different from work. Well, he'd wanted to kiss her, and he had. And he was glad.

He hadn't given a no-strings-attached kiss like that since high school. Stephanie's wounded and fragile air made him extra-cautious. It also drew him to her. Ironically, he only had two months, but he vowed to take things slowly, to give her plenty of leeway. Even if it killed him.

He scratched his chest and paced back and forth across the kitchen. Stephanie was sleek, not flashy; intelligent, but not street-smart. Her hair changed colors in the sun from brown with a hint of red to full-out copper. Her eyes often looked like honey. And she was sweet, in a withdrawn sort of way.

He scraped his jaw. Did any of the description make sense? All he knew for sure was a deep gut reaction happened each and every time he saw her. That was not normal. For him.

What he'd give for a little affectionate nuzzling with her right about now, especially if it quickly evolved into hot and panting sex. But he was going to take it slow. *Remember?* He sloshed back a quick gulp of cold water.

Robbie coughed again.

Phil had already ruled out enlarged adenoids on the kid. He'd played the old airplane spoon of ice cream flying straight for Robbie's mouth, but only if his brother promised to open wide. He'd flashed his penlight across the back of his throat, in the guise of making sure the runway was clear, and all had looked normal in the tonsil and adenoid department, even though Phil must have looked a fool in order to find out. To be honest, it was kind of fun. He was getting a taste of parenting, and realized some of it wasn't so bad.

More muffled coughing drew him back to the guest room. Robbie's butt was up in the air and his thumb had found its way back to his mouth. Some picture. The nasal cannula delivering a small amount of oxygen he'd tried as an experiment had been removed, giving the boy's forehead the concentrated air instead of Robbie's lungs. Phil smiled and shook his head. The stinker really was something. He thought about taking a picture, but he didn't want to risk waking Robbie up so instead he closed the door all but four inches. Besides, taking a picture would be acting like Jon, and he definitely didn't want to go down that path.

Robbie coughed again. Phil ran his hand through his hair, frustrated. He needed to do a bronchoscopy on him, document his condition, and get him started on either CPAP or negative pressure ventilation. Right now the bigger question was, when in his busy clinic schedule would he have time to do one?

An idea popped into his mind and wouldn't let go. Weren't people supposed to face their demons in order to move on? Maybe one small step at a time. Yeah, that might work. If things went as planned, he'd have a coerced but hopefully willing helper on Tuesday evening. How bad could a sedated kid be to be around?

Maybe he'd finally have proof his brother had tracheobronchomalacia. And if he played his cards right, he'd finagle some extra time with the lovely doctor from the desert.

* * *

On Tuesday afternoon, Stephanie sat in her office with a mug of coffee. Staring out the window through the gorgeous lace curtains to the bright blue sky, she contemplated her schedule for the next week—except her mind kept drifting to a certain moment at the beach on Saturday. Okay, so she was out of practice, but was she such a bad kisser that she'd completely turned Phil off?

She'd only caught glimpses of him at the clinic since then, and even though she shouldn't care what he thought about her or her kissing, it made her feel as insecure as if she were still in high school. As if she'd made a mistake by letting him kiss her. But she'd wanted him to.

She took another sip of coffee, loathing the teenaged insecurity, just as Phil appeared at her door, bringing with him a sudden tingle-fest.

"Got any plans for tonight?" he asked.

Why did her mood brighten instantaneously? She had no intention of telling him she'd planned on a little shopping at the Paseo before she took in a movie, alone.

"A few. Nothing major," she said, playing it coy.

One look at his great smile and she wanted to get angry for his turning her world sideways. She wanted to hate him for being so damn charming! But all she could muster was a mental, *Wow, I'd forgotten how gorgeous you are.*

"Would you consider doing me a huge favor?" he asked.

She had nothing better planned, so why not? "Depends." Heck, he'd been the one avoiding her. Why make it easy?

He scratched his chin. "As in what's in it for me, depends?"

"It depends on what you want me to do."

"How about I start by telling you how I'll repay you?" A single dimple appeared.

Oh, he thought he was a smooth operator, but she wasn't that easy. No way. "I don't do bribes, Hansen. No babies, no bribes. Sorry."

He nodded, the second dimple making itself annoyingly visible. "Okay, I'll come clean."

He moved closer and sat on the edge of her

desk. She immediately picked up the scent of his crisp and expensive cologne. An impeccable dresser, his pinstriped shirt and flashy patterned tie was the perfect complement to the dark gray slacks. And, *sheesh*, without even trying, his hair looked great, waving in all the right places, with an unintentional clump falling across his brow.

"It does involve a kid," he said. "My kid brother, to be exact." He raised a finger before she could protest. "But here's the deal. I need to scope his lungs and I need to do it tonight, and I need some extra hands and credentials to make it legal. You in?"

She stared at him.

"It's not like you'd be babysitting. Think of it as a technical procedure, and I need your help. That's all."

"That tracheobronchomalacia business?"

He nodded. "I want to get it documented and refer him for CPAP immediately."

"What about your dad and stepmom?"

"I finally got their verbal consent over the

phone, and while Robbie's with me, I have medical consent."

"I know nothing about pediatric conscious sedation," she said.

"I'll take care of everything. I just need you to monitor Robbie and inject the drugs while I scope him. I'll recover him and you can leave as soon as I'm through."

She considered his request, but made the stupid mistake of glancing into his eyes, which watched and waited and reminded her of the ocean last Saturday at high noon. He ramped up the pressure by tilting his head and giving a puppy-dog can-we-take-a-walk expression. If Phil handled everything, and all she had to do was administer drugs and do the technical monitoring, maybe she could help him out.

"What time?"

"I've got to pick him up from day care in ten minutes. Mmm, how about in half an hour?"

That didn't give her much time to think it over, or change her mind. She pulled out her drawer and, having learned from her snack expedition the other night with Robbie, found a pack of peanut butter with cheese crackers, tore it open with her teeth, and tossed the first one into her mouth.

"You're on," she said, sounding muffled.

As naturally as old friends, he kissed her cheek. "You're the best," he said, and took off, leaving her chomping on her snack, blowing cracker flakes from her mouth when she sighed. And there was that damn feeling he brought along with him every time they talked—flustered.

The new and state-of-the-art procedure suite at Midcoast Medical provided the perfect setting for Robbie's examination. Jason had had the equipment installed after a successful second-quarter report. Every penny they made beyond salaries went right back into their clinic with upgrades and added services. Phil no longer had to rent space at the local hospital to perform his bronchoscopies, taking him away from the clinic, and making his nurse able to increase her hours to full-time as a result.

But this examination was after hours, and

he'd lined up a great replacement for his regular nurse—Stephanie.

She hadn't bargained on Robbie being awake when she arrived, and Phil had to do some quick talking to make her stick around.

"I can't do this on my own, Stephanie. Please. Five minutes. It will only take five minutes. I promise."

She looked pale and hesitated at the procedure-room door, but something, maybe it was Robbie looking so vulnerable and unsuspecting, made her change her mind.

Robbie fought like the devil when Phil tried to insert an intravenous line, and he thought she'd bolt right then and there. Surprisingly, she held the boy's arm steady, and with her help they got the IV in and the keep-open solution running. She'd been an unexpected decoy with her medley of wacky kids' songs. Robbie even giggled a few times. If she didn't do kids, how did she know all those children's songs?

Gowned, gloved and masked, Phil watched Stephanie draw up the quick-acting, deeply sedating medication. He knew there was a fine line between true anesthesia and conscious sedation, and though he wanted to make Robbie comfortable, he didn't want him too sedated, just out of it long enough to get a minitour inside his lungs. After she had set up Robbie with pulse oximetry, heart and blood-pressure monitor, and supplemental oxygen, he directed her to give the standard pediatric dose for fentanyl and benzodiapine instead of a newer, short-acting drug.

"No offense, but I only use Propofol when I have an anesthesiologist working with me." He smiled at her through his mask.

She tossed him a sassy look. "Believe me, no offense taken, I already feel out of my element here." With skilled and efficient hands she titrated the drugs into the IV as he applied the topical numbing spray to Robbie's throat, and within seconds Robbie drifted into twilight sleep.

"I called ahead to the preschool to hold his lunch, but Robbie loves to eat so much he almost snuck a snack around three today. Fortunately, they caught him, so we shouldn't have a problem with emesis." He flipped on the suction machine, using his elbow to protect his sterile gloves. This would be his backup contingency plan in case Robbie did vomit.

"I'm going to use a pediatric laryngeal mask airway instead of an endotracheal tube." He showed her the small spoon-shaped device. "As Robbie has the typical shortened Down syndrome neck, an endotracheal tube would have been tricky anyway," he said as he lubricated the tablespoon-size silicone mask and slipped the tube inside Robbie's slack mouth. The boy didn't flinch. "See? I don't even need a laryngoscope with this gizmo."

Once the LMA was in place, Phil immediately reached for his bronchoscope and slipped the flexible tube down Robbie's trachea for a quick look-see.

"See that?" he said to Stephanie, who took turns intently watching the procedure on the digital TV screen, keeping track of the heart and BP monitor readings, and watching Robbie in the flesh. Sure enough, due to softened cartilage, his trachea showed signs of floppiness and collapsed while he breathed under the sedation. The same thing happened while he slept each night. "This is classic TBM." Keeping things short and sweet, and already having digitally recorded his findings, Phil removed the scope and quickly followed suit with the laryngeal mask airway. Even though sedated, Robbie coughed and sputtered. "All the kid needs is continuous positive airway pressure while he sleeps, so he won't have to cough every time his trachea collapses."

"That's great news," Stephanie said, watching Robbie like an anxious mother hen.

True to the short-life drug effect, Robbie started to come out of his stupor. "There you go, buddy, we're all done," Phil said. He bent over and looked into his blinking eyes. "Are you in there somewhere?"

The bleary-eyed Robbie tried to look in the vicinity of his voice. Phil set the scope on the counter and prepared to wipe it clean before putting it in the sterilization solution overnight.

"Can you watch him a few minutes while I clean up?" he asked.

She nodded, undoing her mask and letting it hang around her neck, though keeping a safe distance from Robbie.

As with many recently sedated children, Robbie woke up confused, fussing and crying. Phil worked as quickly as he could. "You're okay, Rob. I'm right here, buddy," he said. The boy seemed to calm down immediately. Phil smiled, assuming the sound of his voice had done the trick, but when he glanced over his shoulder, he saw a sight that made him smile even wider.

The I-don't-do-kids doctor was holding Robbie's hand and patting it.

"You at all interested in getting takeout and keeping me company tonight while I help my kid brother recover from major surgery?" He'd lay it on thick, and hope for the best.

She remained quiet for a few seconds, then let go of Robbie's hand.

"I can't, Phil. I'm sorry."

* * *

On Wednesday morning, Stephanie hung up the phone after a long conversation with her mother. She'd used the excuse of being on call—which wasn't completely untrue—for not showing for Thanksgiving. If things followed the usual routine, her sister would be on the phone within the next ten minutes, and Mary was ruthless when it came to arm-twisting. All the more reason to get started with her appointments.

Phil had surprised her last night with both his technical skill and tender banter with his brother. The more she got to know him, the more she suspected his playboy reputation was just a cover. Helping out with Robbie's exam hadn't been nearly as bad as she'd thought it would be, another surprise. Maybe she was getting used to him. She'd watched the boy sleep, and yearning had clutched her heart. If only her son could be alive.

She closed her eyes and bit her lip. Someone tapped on the door.

"Your next patient is ready."

Thank heavens for work.

By midmorning, Amy delivered the latest batch of lab reports and special tests.

Stephanie shuffled through the stack with an eye out for two in particular. The first was great news—it was just an ovarian cyst for Ms. Winkler. The next report wasn't nearly as welcome. Celeste Conroy's Pap smear showed abnormal cells. She picked up the phone.

After she'd calmed the woman down, she suggested her plan. "I'd like to perform a colposcopy, which is a fancy way of looking at your cervix up close with a bright light and magnifying glass."

The proactive next step went over better than the bombshell dysplasia news.

"And while I'm examining your cervix, I'll take a tiny biopsy of that questionable area. This will give us a better idea of exactly what we're dealing with."

After a brief silence, several questions flew from the young pregnant woman's mouth. Stephanie answered each as she was able.

"The exam is not threatening to your pregnancy, though after I do the biopsy, there may be some mild cramping and light bleeding. We'd have to monitor you carefully to make sure the bleeding was from the biopsy and not from the pregnancy, but the risk is extremely low that your baby will be in jeopardy."

After a few more minutes of convincing the patient to arrange an appointment on Friday, the day after Thanksgiving, she hung up.

And now she had a good reason to stay in Santa Barbara for Thanksgiving. She needed to be well rested and in top form on Friday. Mary could twist her arm all she wanted, but she wouldn't give in to Thanksgiving dinner in the desert.

Her next call was pure pleasure. "Ms. Winkler? This is Dr. Bennett from Midcoast Medical. I've got your ultrasound results back, and you can rest assured that your enlarged ovary is nothing more than a pesky cyst."

She smiled when her patient sang out a loud "Hallelujah!"

By lunchtime it occurred to Stephanie that she hadn't seen Phil in the clinic all morning. She nibbled at her microwaved plate of food, and halfheartedly chatted with a couple of coworkers. It also occurred to her that Thanksgiving was going to be one lonely day. She'd hole up in her hotel room and watch a stack of old DVDs and pretend it was just another day. Maybe she'd eat an open-faced turkey sandwich with dressing and gravy, with a side of cranberries from the deli around the corner, too. Oh, and she'd watch the famous New York Thanksgiving Day parade on TV, she mused with a jumble of faraway thoughts.

"I bet you're wondering where I've been," Phil said, standing beside her.

"What makes you think I've even noticed?" she said, glancing over her shoulder, going along with his playful tone.

"*We* noticed you weren't around," one of the two nurses sharing the community lounge table chimed in. As far as Stephanie could tell, Phil had all the ladies in the clinic wrapped around his finger.

His quirked brow and goofy expression of "see what I'm saying?" made her laugh. It felt good.

"Thank you, Tamara and Stacy," he said. "I'm glad someone noticed."

He sat next to Stephanie, edging out Jon's nurse, though there was plenty of room on the other side of the table, then unpacked a couple of shrimp tacos from his brown bag. "You know, that's what I like about you. You're not under my spell."

She almost spat out her soda. "You have a spell?" She was walking on thin ice because she knew without a doubt he did have a special something that very well could be called a spell, and that she was most likely already under it… especially since their kiss.

"So I've been told."

"He's got a spell," the nurses said together.

She laughed and shook her head. "Well, I don't know about a spell, but I do know you've got a jelly stain on your shirt."

He pulled in his chin and glanced downward. "Oh, that. It's probably from when I made Robbie's sandwich this morning."

With each day, and all the little details she noticed about him, Phil became more irresistible.

Not that she was interested or anything. "So where were you?"

"Where else? The preschool. Seems like it's my second home. How does Roma do it?"

"Don't let this go to your head, Phil, but I think you're doing a pretty good job of pinch-hitting for your parents."

"They're due back tonight, and I'm counting the hours."

The nurses finished their lunch, and announced they were just about to take a walk before the afternoon clinic opened when René Munroe appeared, complete with swaddled baby in her arms and Jon at her side.

"Hi, Dr. Munroe!" one of the nurses said, rushing over to look at the newborn. "Oh, he's adorable. May I hold him?"

"Sure," the dark-haired René said, glowing with new-mom pride.

Phil popped up and took a peek under the blanket. "Hey, he looks just like those pictures."

René rolled her eyes. "Oh, gosh, has Jon been boring everyone with pictures?"

Phil nodded, but the nurses quickly protested, "No! We love baby pictures."

"Oh, hey, René, this is Stephanie Bennett, the doc we hired to cover your patients," Jon said, looking a bit abashed and obviously wanting to change the subject.

They greeted each other and Stephanie already felt as though she knew René from working in her office. While Jon passed the baby around, Stephanie discussed Celeste Conroy's abnormal Pap smear with René and her plans for following up. When René agreed with the next step, Stephanie felt much more confident.

"Would you like me to call and reassure her that I'm in total agreement?" René said.

"That would be wonderful."

"Okay, last chance to hold Evan before I take René out to lunch," Jon said, having taken back his son but seeming ready to share him with anyone who wanted. "Stephanie?"

He offered the teddy-bear-patterned bundle of blanket to her and she froze. Oh, no, what should she do? Would it be completely awkward to refuse? Her pulse sputtered in her chest, and her ears rang. She liked these people and didn't want to insult them.

"Okay," she said, feigning a smile. She held Evan with stiff arms, away from her chest. "Aren't you something?" Memories of her son gurgling and cooing hit so fast and hard she found it impossible to breathe. She blinked back the images as her heart stumbled, and she handed the baby back to René, trying her best to disguise her quivery voice. "You must be so proud."

The huge, beaming smile on René's face gave the answer. She cuddled the baby to her heart and kissed his cheek. "I wuv this wittle guy."

Jon laughed and scratched his nose. "Anyone know a cure for a highly educated woman who suddenly starts talking baby talk?"

The nurses giggled. "It's a requirement of motherhood, Doc," one of them said.

Flushed and edgy, Stephanie willed her hands to stop shaking. She'd looked into those beautiful baby gray eyes and had seen Justin. She'd glanced up to find Phil intently watching her as her lungs clutched at each breath.

Somehow she made it through the goodbyes, but as soon as the couple left she headed for the back door and the tranquil promise of the yard. She needed to breathe, to get hold of herself.

She was staring at the small bubbling fountain and listening to chattering birds in the tree when a hand grasped her arm. It was Phil. He'd picked up on what had just happened. Hell, she'd been so obvious, anyone would have noticed her fumbling attempt at acting normal…if they hadn't been so distracted with the baby.

"I was wondering what you're doing tomorrow," he said.

She welcomed the change in subject, even if it was another sticky topic. How should she best phrase the fact she had no plans for Thanksgiving and not come off as pitiful? Sure, she could go to Palm Desert, but it wasn't going to happen.

She swallowed and said, "I'm having a quiet day."

He glanced thoughtfully at her. "My stepmother

is a fantastic cook, and she promised me a Thanksgiving dinner to die for as I've been taking care of Robbie and all, and I thought you might like to be my plus one."

"Plus one?"

"My guest. What do you say? Great food. Even better company. You'll like my dad." He tilted his head, and his crescent-shaped eyes looked very inviting. "Robbie will be so happy to see them that he'll leave you alone. I promise." Phil was the distraction she needed—a guy completely unaware of her past, who didn't ask questions, and with one not-so-subtle thing on his mind.

Did she really need to think about it? Hotel room. DVDs. Deli sandwich. Or plus one.

"You know what? I'd really like that."

The full-out smile he delivered assured her she'd not only made the right decision but she'd also made his afternoon. When in the past three years had she been able to make that claim about a man? And it felt pretty darn good.

He looked as if he wanted to kiss her again, and maybe that's exactly what she needed right now, a kiss to make her forget, but his beeper went off and after a quick glance, a forlorn look replaced the charm. He sighed. "It's the preschool, again."

Late that afternoon, Phil appeared at Stephanie's office door, looking agitated.

"What's up?" she asked.

"The damn weather."

She glanced out her window at another perfectly clear blue autumn sky then back at Phil. "Looks pretty good to me."

"I'm talking about Maui. They're having a terrible storm and the return flight has been canceled until Friday. Looks like Thanksgiving dinner is off."

She couldn't deny the disappointment. Ever since he'd invited her, she'd felt a buzz of expectation, a curiosity about his family, and mouthwatering anticipation of great food. Now a storm on a tropical island had changed everything. "How disappointing…for them. I'm sure they're eager to get home to Robbie and all."

He snapped his fingers. "I've got an idea. Come to my house and I'll order a turkey dinner." His eyes lit up. "It'll be fun, and you can help me warm things up. What do you say?

She'd swung from one end of the emotional pendulum to the opposite over this Thanksgiving, and here was yet a new twist. Hotel. DVDs. Deli sandwich. Or spend an afternoon with a gorgeous guy…and Robbie?

It all came down to one desire. Did she want to have a life again? Or go on living in a vacuum. Hotel. DVDs. Deli sandwich…or…

There really wasn't a decision to make. "What time?"

CHAPTER FIVE

ON THANKSGIVING morning, Stephanie put extra effort into getting dressed. She wanted to look good, but not overdo it. She opted for casual with jeans and boots, a pumpkin-colored top with a flashy hip belt, and a multi-fall-colored knit scarf to ward off the cooler weather.

She'd stopped last night at the bakery she'd recently discovered and got one of the last two pumpkin pies baked that afternoon, the kind of whipped cream you sprayed from a can, and a bottle of deep red wine to go with the turkey. She had no intention of impressing Phil with her culinary skills. Heck, she was living in a hotel, how could she? And wasn't he the one who'd invited her to dinner?

She arrived at his house just before noon, impressed with the rolling brown hills and secluded homes scattered across them. The sprawling country farmhouse was the last type of home she'd expect to see Phil living in. In the distance, and far behind her, the ocean sparkled as if the bold sun had scattered glitter over it. She took a deep breath of fresh air, savoring the special view, suddenly aware that her insides were letting go of that usual tight knot.

Santa Barbara had a completely different kind of beauty from the tall purple mountains that encased her desert home, and the flat breadth between them. Both were special, but the ocean added that extra touch with which, in her opinion, no amount of saguaro cactus or Joshua trees could compete.

With an odd sense of contentment folding in around her, she tapped lightly on his door before ringing the bell. After a short time the door swung open, with Phil grinning and with Robbie riding piggyback.

"Hey," he said, a little breathless. "Come in."

The spacious living room, with a stone fireplace and wall-long French doors and windows, was bright and open. The light-colored hardwood floors were offset by high, dark beamed and arched ceilings. The family room opened into a modern kitchen complete with cooking island and expensive-looking Italian tile floors.

Toys were everywhere. Pillows and books were scattered around the family room, and furniture was obviously askew.

Phil looked happy, and for a confirmed bachelor he was doing a fine job at playing stand-in father. "We were just horsing around, weren't we, shorty?"

Robbie giggled and nodded, and once Phil released him, he ran off toward a beach ball, blissfully unaware of Stephanie invading his territory.

Maybe she was getting used to being around Robbie, because he hadn't set off any internal alarms today. Or maybe she was distracted by the attractive guy right in front of her. He wore jeans and a white tailored Western-styled shirt with the collar open, revealing a hint of light brown chest hair. And he kept smiling at her, his white straight teeth like something out of a maga-zine ad.

"You look great," he said. "As always."

The compliment stopped her. At the end of her marriage her husband had thought she was despicable. Couldn't stand to look at her and hadn't minded telling her so. Knowing that, on top of every horrible thought she'd already had about herself, had almost made her lose the will to live. She shook her head, refusing to go there again. She wanted to move forward and she couldn't very well do that by constantly looking over her shoulder, remembering the bad times.

Phil had just told her she looked great. Did he tell all his dates that? "Thank you." She felt her cheeks heat up.

"I mean it." He pinned her with a no-nonsense gaze.

"I believe you." Did she? Did she have the nerve to tell him how fantastic he looked, too?

"Good."

The antsy feeling made her need to change the subject. "This house is amazing," she said.

"Thanks. I've only been here a couple of years, but I like to call it home."

"Oh, here's the pie and some other stuff," she said.

He took her few items into the kitchen, reading the wine label on the way. Instead of sitting, she followed him, sliding her hand over the cool granite countertops and marveling at the state-of-the-art stainless-steel appliances. This was the kind of home a person dreamed about but never intended to actually live in. And what was a bachelor like Phil doing here?

"This seems so unlike you," she said.

"Tell that to my Realtor. I spent a year looking for it. This is the place I intend to stay in."

"A guy like you?"

"Hey, give me a break. I may not be interested in settling down, but a house, well, I have no qualms about where I want to live for the rest of my life."

"We really don't know a thing about each other, do we?" she said, smiling.

His eyes brightened to daylight blue. "Here's

something else to surprise you." He washed his hands and opened a cupboard. "I'm cooking today."

The undeniable aroma of turkey hit her nostrils. "I thought you were ordering in?"

"I got to thinking, how hard could cooking a turkey be? My butcher gave me instructions, and they didn't sound difficult."

How many more surprises did he have up his sleeve? "Well, it smells great."

"Hey, you're gonna love the dressing. I made Roma fax the recipe to me last night."

She laughed. For the first time in ages, she felt excited about Thanksgiving.

He washed a few vegetables in the sink. "What would you like to drink?"

"Water is fine." Heaven forbid she should have a glass of wine, relax, and let her guard down.

He delivered her a glass as she sat on one of the stools by the island. "You've got to admit this beats eating in your hotel room, right?"

She gazed across the comfortable and stylish home and nodded. "You win. Hands down, this beats my hotel. I feel like I'm in a *House Beautiful* commercial."

He smiled, obviously liking her description of his home.

"These are from my garden." He held up a handful of new carrots, and medium-size tomatoes.

"You're kidding me," she said. "You garden, too?"

"What can I say? I like being in the sun. I like digging in the dirt and pulling weeds. Don't tell anyone at work, they'd never let me live it down."

"Your secret's safe with me," she said, taking a sip of water and fighting off an ever-growing crush on her surprising host.

"How are you at mashing potatoes?" he asked, just as something hit the back of her butt with a plunk. She jerked around, it was the beach ball, and Robbie had a guilty expression on his face.

"Hey, remember what I said about throwing that thing around in here," Phil chided Robbie.

"Outside, Pill," the boy said. "Go. Peez?"

"I'm busy right now."

"Now!" Robbie said, throwing the ball at Stephanie and hitting her stomach this time.

"Okay, mister, you're in big trouble." Phil headed for Robbie, who didn't take him seriously in the least. The boy must have thought they were playing catch-me-if-you-can, as he ran off on short, squat legs, no chance of escaping Phil's reach.

Phil grabbed him by the collar then held him over his hip. Robbie kicked and griped. Phil glanced at Stephanie, his embarrassment obvious. "Sometimes I just can't control this kid."

"Tell you what," she said, trying not to smile as Robbie continued to squeal with delight. She had half an urge to toss the ball back to him, even though it was against the rules, but Phil was setting limits and she didn't want to confuse the boy. "I'll peel the potatoes while you two work off some extra energy."

"Sounds like a plan." He nodded with a grateful glance. "Okay, buster, you're gonna get what for," he said with mock seriousness.

"No!" Robbie said. "*You're* gonna get what for!"

Stephanie couldn't help but smile. She watched momentarily as they headed outside, an odd sensation taking hold. Ignoring the nudge toward a change of heart, she headed for the kitchen.

Phil's house was laid out so that the kitchen flowed directly into the family room, and the family room opened to a patio, and beyond that the huge expanse of verdant yard was accented by flowering hibiscus in white and red and assorted leafy bushes. From the large ranch-style kitchen windows she could see their wild game of catch or dodge-the-beach-ball or whatever their version of "what for" was called. Seemed as if all Phil's griping about being stuck with his kid brother for ten days was nothing more than a cover. And Robbie was having the time of his life, laughing, throwing, and running all over the place. Looked like kid's heaven to her. And Phil played the role of a benevolent uncle wanting nothing more than to make the kid happy.

Happy.

That was a word that had slipped from her vocabulary these past three years. As she peeled the potatoes, sliced and dropped them into a bowl of cold water, she pondered how inviting the old and nearly forgotten feeling was. Her lips stretched into a broad smile that reached like a warm glove into her chest and squeezed her heart. Welcome back to the living. Happy felt great.

It hit her before the next breath. She'd admitted being happy and she was in the company of a little boy. Wow. Maybe things were finally breaking through that guilt logjam.

Robbie was a sweet kid. Justin was a memory she'd always hold deep in her heart and never forget, but Robbie wasn't Justin. She wasn't Robbie's mother. She wasn't responsible for him. Why be afraid of him? Did she want to spend the rest of her life cowering around *all* children, or was it finally time to face her fear?

She wiped her hands on the dish towel and walked toward the French doors. As she opened them and walked onto the patio, she swallowed and took a steadying breath. "Um…" Her gaze darted around the yard as she picked at her nails.

Phil quit jogging and gave her an odd look. "Is everything okay?"

Her hand flew to her hair. "Yeah. Um…I was just wondering…"

He took a few steps toward her, a concerned expression clouding his good looks. At the moment, passing the medical boards seemed easier than what she wanted to say. Another deep breath.

"Do you have room for one more in that game?"

By the time the potatoes had boiled, Phil had followed Stephanie back to the kitchen. Robbie looked sufficiently pooped out and sat in front of a children's DVD in his little corner of the family room. On a separate large-screen TV the annual Thanksgiving Texas football game was going on.

"I'd better put the yams in the oven," Phil said. "I got this dish from my caterer."

She glanced over her shoulder at the gorgeous-looking casserole complete with pecans on top. Phil opened a top oven, slid the dish inside then checked on the turkey in the lower oven, basting it as if he'd done this before.

"You're making my mouth water," she said, savoring the smell. She'd worked up quite an appetite running around with Robbie and Phil. And it hadn't wiped her out emotionally either. If anything, it had invigorated her.

"It'll be done in another half hour. In the meantime, I'm having a beer. Can I get you anything?"

Could she even remember the last time she'd had a glass of wine? "I'll try that wine I brought."

"You're on."

By the time they'd set the table, made the gravy, and laid out all the food, the few sips of wine she'd managed to find time to take had already gone to her head. The pleasant buzz filtered throughout her body, heating her insides and causing her to smile. A lot. How could a few sips of wine make her feel that giddy? Maybe this great feeling had a lot more to do with Phil, Robbie, and Thanksgiving than the liquid spirits. She took another sip, loving the way the simply laid-out table looked, and before he signaled for her to sit, she grabbed her purse.

"Wait," she said. "I want to take a picture of this. It's so beautiful." She dug out her cell phone and snapped first a picture of the turkey in the center of the table, then had Robbie and Phil pose for one, heads close to the bird. Then she snapped one of herself at arm's length with the two of them beside her and the turkey in the background. In her opinion, all three were keepers, even if the third one, taken at such close range, looked as if they all had oversize noses and heads.

Things had been so busy all afternoon she hadn't allowed herself to examine Phil's proximity to her until now as they studied her photographs. She felt his warmth and it called to her. Reacting before thinking, she turned and reached for him, gave him a hug, and kissed his cheek.

"Thank you so much for inviting me," she said, a little bit of her heart going out of her. Though frightening at first, his welcoming reception gave her courage not to pull back inside. Maybe

Phil was someone she could let her hair down around.

"I'm really glad you're here," he said with a sincere glint in his eyes, as if on the verge of kissing her.

"Pill! Eat!"

He rolled his eyes. "Can you imagine how hard it would have been to keep him entertained all afternoon by myself?"

She laughed. He'd given her a compliment then quickly yanked it back.

"Eat now!" Robbie chanted.

"Right," he said. "First order of business."

Once everyone was seated at the table, and their plates were filled, Phil surprised her even more. "Robbie? Will you say grace for us?" He looked at her and winked. "I got a note from preschool saying they've been practicing."

The boy's big brown eyes grew serious. He licked his lips a couple of times, obviously considering what to say, then he clamped his lids together. "Thank you for da peshell food. For my fambly. For Pill. And for Theff-oh-nee."

With her head bowed, big fat tears brimmed as Stephanie blinked and whispered, "Amen."

Thanksgiving dinner had gone better than Phil could possibly have dreamed. After they'd worn him out playing ball, Robbie was on his best behavior. And Phil had almost fallen over when Stephanie had asked if she could join in. She'd chased Robbie around the yard as if she were a kid again, as if it didn't bother her anymore to be around him. After the panic he'd caused her that first night, this was an amazing improvement.

Dinner was exceptional, if he did say so himself. Not one thing got burned, except for the crescent rolls, and that was only a little on the bottoms. They were still edible, especially if you loaded them up with sweetened cranberry sauce straight from the caterer.

Stephanie was more animated than he'd ever seen her. It brightened those gorgeous eyes and made her prettier than he'd previously thought, dazzling him with her easy charm. Too bad his eyelids were at half-mast and his stomach so full that he didn't have the energy to get up and walk across the room to plant a kiss on her. If he didn't move in the next few seconds he'd fall asleep. Some impression that would make.

"You sit, and I'll clean up," she said. "It's the least I can do."

He thought about protesting, but the couch felt great and it was the third quarter in the game and Dallas was only ahead by a field goal. Robbie crawled up and snuggled beside him. That did it. "Thanks!"

By the time Stephanie had finished the dishes, Phil and Robbie had fallen asleep. The sight of the two of them on the couch sent a chill through her heart. A memory flashed of her holding her baby, exhausted, eyelids heavy, the couch inviting her to settle down and rest, just for a moment...

Didn't Phil know how dangerous that was? A pop of adrenaline drove her to rush to the sofa. She delicately lifted Robbie so as not to wake him or disturb Phil. She couldn't very well hold him as if he had a dirty diaper and expect him to stay asleep, so she brought him to her chest. On automatic pilot, Robbie wrapped his legs around her waist, and hung his arms over her shoulders. She anchored him beneath his bottom and across his back, and he nuzzled his head against her neck. A rush of motherly feelings made her feel dizzy. He was so much heavier and bigger than Justin, her four-month-old baby.

She hugged Robbie tight and, determined not to succumb to her woozy feeling, walked carefully down the hall to his room. She could do this. It was time to prove she could.

As she prepared him for his nap, his sublime expression sent her thoughts to Justin. He'd always looked like an angel when he'd slept. *Sweetheart, Mommy will always love you. Please forgive me.*

She bit her lip and fought the pinpricks behind her lids as she wondered how different her life would have been if she'd put her baby to bed that night. Today, through Robbie, she'd pretend she had…

At some point Phil had drifted off to sleep, and the next thing he remembered was a cool hand on his cheek. Her hand. The faint feel of her fingers reminded him of butterfly wings, delicate and beautiful, and easily harmed. Strangely, it made him want to look out for her in the same odd way he wanted to protect Robbie.

He must have stretched out on the couch because she sat on the edge, facing him.

"Are you ready for dessert?" she asked, sending a thought through his brain completely different from what she'd probably intended. "I've made some coffee."

Ah, that dessert.

Through his bleary eyes, her familiar butterscotch-and-cream features came into focus. Without thinking, he took her hand and kissed her slender fingers. "I'd love some," he said, thinking more about what he'd really like right then.

Heat radiated from his gaze, and half of her mouth hitched into a knowing smile as she edged away. "Don't move. I'll bring it to you."

As he woke up a little more, he got suddenly curious. "Where's Robbie?" He sat bolt upright, a sudden knot of concern lodged in his chest.

"He fell asleep, too. I hope you don't mind, but I put him to bed."

"You put him to bed? How long have I been out?"

"An hour, give or take a few minutes."

He scrubbed his face. "Man, some host I am."

"You've been a perfect host," she said, on her way to the kitchen, practically skipping. This was a side of Stephanie he'd never seen, and definitely liked. She'd come outside and played with him and Robbie, though it had felt like pulling teeth to get her to ask. She'd shared Thanksgiving with them, as if they were a small and happy family— this from the woman who hadn't been able to go near them in the Japanese restaurant. And now she'd put Robbie to bed.

While she was busy preparing coffee and dessert in the kitchen, he wandered down the hall to Robbie's room. The door had been left a few inches open, like Roma had instructed Phil the first night she'd left him. Robbie slept peacefully…in his blanket sleeper.

What kind of a woman would think to put him

in his pajamas and leave the door ajar? He thought about some of the women he'd dated over the past year. He'd bet his house that none of them would have thought of it. Hell, they'd probably have left him right on the couch where they'd found him, but not Stephanie.

Phil scratched his head as he exited the bedroom, leaving the door as he'd found it. Who would be that considerate?

A mother, that was who.

Was Stephanie a mother? Then why would she freak out around kids? And if she was a mother, where was her child? Maybe she'd been through a bad divorce, and her husband had gotten custody. Nah, that seemed too outrageous. The woman was a doctor and a great person. Sometimes disgruntled husbands kidnapped their kids. He shook his head, unable to go there, but something tormented her and he intended to find out what it was.

He glanced into the kitchen, at Stephanie pottering around, whistling under her breath. She'd come out of her shell today. He'd just begun to glimpse a different side of Stephanie Bennett, and he liked what he'd discovered. Even with all of his questions, Thanksgiving wasn't a day to dig up her past. He didn't want to spoil her upbeat mood; the lady deserved a break.

A subtle smoothness to her brow made him think she'd made peace with herself today, that maybe she'd conquered a demon or two, and he was glad to witness it.

She looked great, too. Those straight-leg jeans hugged her hips in all the right places, and the silky top revealed the hint of a soft, sweet cleavage. And her hair. What could he say about that gorgeous head of hair, other than he'd love to get his fingers tangled up in it?

By the time he sat down, she showed up with two cups of coffee, handing him one and sitting on the edge of the sofa again. "As I said, you're a fantastic host. I haven't felt this relaxed in ages. Besides, that's the beauty of a huge turkey dinner in the afternoon. You get to nap and wake up in time for a sandwich later." There was that bright smile again. "Oh, and Dallas won."

"Go, Cowboys!" What was it about her smile that drove him over the edge? From this closer range the fine sprinkling of freckles he'd discovered across her nose looked the exact color of her hair. She was a vision he thought he'd never get tired of, and he wanted to hold her, to feel her hair on his face, to kiss those freckles, but he was holding a hot cup of coffee instead.

They'd had a great afternoon together, really gotten to know each other better, and he liked every single thing he'd discovered.

She sat next to him with her leg curled under her. She'd slipped off her shoes, and he noticed polished toenails that matched her top. A fleeting image of her in a bath towel, painting her nails, sent a quick thrill through his veins. He wanted her, pure and simple. He wanted to make love to her, to make her come alive.

No risk, no gain.

He set the cup down, and reached for her. "Come here," he said.

Surprise flickered in her eyes. She put her cup on the table and with no sign of resistance snuggled into his arms. He kissed her cheek then brushed her mouth with his thumb. "You have no idea how much I want to kiss you," he said.

She tasted his thumb. He saw a flash of fire in those butterscotch depths. There wasn't any question what her answer was. She tilted her chin to make better contact as their mouths came together.

He picked up where he'd left off at the beach, slipping his tongue between her soft lips, and found her velvet-slick mouth.

She cupped his face and kissed him hard. He delved deeper, ravenous for her taste, then mated his tongue with hers. They made love with their mouths as time ceased to exist. He had no idea how long they'd necked, all he knew was that she matched his heated response, pressing her body against his, smothering him with her lips. He knew where needy kisses like that led, and there was no going back.

The fine skin of her neck tasted like vanilla. She moaned as if he'd uncovered the most sensual spot on her body. He wanted to explore more, discover every area that drove her mad with desire, but she was fully clothed. He'd have to fix that. Immediately. He cupped her breast, and felt the tightened nipple under the thin fabric of her top. His ears were so hot he thought they might spontaneously combust, and his now-full erection pulsed and strained to be set free.

As difficult as it was, he broke away from her fired-up kisses, stood, and took her hand. "Follow me."

With flushed cheeks and hooded eyes, eyes that confirmed she wanted him as much as he wanted her, she followed him down the long hall.

Stephanie watched Phil throw back the covers of his bed and step toward her. He took her by the neck and kissed her so hard she thought her knees would go wobbly.

This was no time to change her mind. Her mind? Hell, she'd misplaced that right around the time he'd kissed her. If she was going to change her mind it had to be now, but desire shivered through her and the only thing in the world she wanted at this moment was to make love with him. She was on fire. A feeling she hadn't experienced in three years pulsed between her legs, and one thing was very clear. Phil wanted her as much as she wanted him.

Hadn't she been telling herself to start living again? Every sensation coursing over her skin and through her veins shouted, *Do it! Give yourself permission*. Phil's mouth clamped down on hers again, and the no-brainer decision was made.

Completely giving in to the moment, she found a way under his shirt and skimmed the taut muscles on his chest, her hands skating across his substantial shoulders. It had been so long since she'd touched a man this way. She savored the feel of naked flesh. His skin was smooth with a fine sprinkling of hair on his chest, and she wanted to see him. See all of him.

"Let me help you," he said, pulling his shirt over his head, buttons untouched.

She only had time to glimpse his flat stomach and defined arms before he did the disappearing act with her top. A hot rhythm between her thighs drove her to undo his jeans. He yanked them down and stepped out, his erection outlined through his black briefs. With a rush of desire she cupped the full length of him, restless to see him, to feel him inside her.

To feel. Him. She'd been living on anxiety and tension for so long, this surge of lust intoxicated her. Every cell in her body came to life, heightening his touch and sweetening his taste. It empowered her, made her think she could do anything. With Phil. She pulled his briefs down and watched as he stepped out of them. She'd seen his physique in the wet suit the other day, but it couldn't compare to him in the flesh. His powerful legs and full erection was a picture she'd hold in her memory for the rest of her life.

With a dark, hooded stare, Phil studied her. "Your turn," he said. He brushed his warm hands over her breasts, cupping and lifting them as he dropped feathery kisses on her shoulder, and expertly unlatched her bra. "You're beautiful. So beautiful," he said in a hushed, reverent tone, kissing each breast.

Their mouths came together again, his lips full and smooth, as they dropped onto the bed. He unzipped and removed her jeans and lacy thong that matched her bra. "Cute," he said, eyebrows lifted in approval as he tossed it across the room. It landed on a lampshade.

Phil's natural banter and easygoing manner helped her relax when she briefly felt out of her depth. What the hell was she doing, having sex with a coworker, with a man known for being a playboy? But she looked into Phil's eyes, saw unadulterated desire, and lost her train of thought. Again.

Today she needed to be desired. It was a truth she could face, a gift he offered, and she had every intention of accepting and savoring it.

They rolled together into the center of his huge bed, finally feeling every part of each other. The exquisite feel of his muscles and skin fanned the flames licking in her belly. They kissed and tasted, touched and kneaded each other until she was frantic. "Please," she said, taking him in her hand and placing him between her thighs. She touched her tongue to his, and nibbled his kiss-swollen lower lip. "I need you," she said.

From the flashing depths of his eyes there was no doubt he needed her, too.

"Let me get some protection," he said with a bedroom-husky voice.

"Not necessary. My tubes are tied," she said, pulling him closer.

He cocked his head as if momentarily surprised, but it didn't stop Phil from seizing the moment and making her needful wishes his complete command.

CHAPTER SIX

STEPHANIE crawled out of her postsex haze and glanced at the surfing god beside her. She couldn't believe what she'd just done—she'd slept with a man after only knowing him for a couple of weeks. Was she out of her mind?

She'd let him tug her down the hall to his bedroom and have his way with her. Now nestled in the crook of his arm, she blinked. Come to think of it, she'd pretty much had her way with him, too. Maybe that was the freedom that having her tubes tied had finally given her. She'd never forget this night, no matter what happened next, and that realization felt great.

He definitely knew how to satisfy a woman, yet he was anything but mechanical or practiced. What they'd shared had been nothing short of fan-bleeping-tastic. When he'd filled her, she'd let herself go with basic instincts and savored each and every sensation coiling tighter and tighter until release had torpedoed through her. Now feeling like a huge mound of jelly, she admitted how much she'd needed this. How glad she was he'd taken her there.

They snuggled warmly in the center of his king-sized bed, lights dimmed, breathing roughly, completely satisfied. Now that he'd had her, he still hadn't lost interest. No. He folded her into his chest—his muscular chest brushed with light brown swirls and curls—and stroked her hair. She loved the soap-and-sex smell of his skin and marveled at how smooth it was and how substantial he felt. She smiled against his chest, her hand on his upper thigh. Phil was definitely substantial.

His fingers lightly played with her matted hair, sending chills over her shoulders. She'd thought she was tingled out, but his touch settled that debate. When she looked up at him, a grin was on his flushed face. He'd had a workout, too.

It had been so long since she'd been with anyone, wasn't this the point where the first-time lovers were supposed to feel awkward and clumsy? She felt anything but as she shared a completely contented smile with him. There wasn't a hint of regret in his clear-as-the-sky eyes.

"I've been fascinated with your hair since the moment I met you," he said, honey-voiced, giving her shivers all over again.

Truth was she'd been fascinated with his hair, too. She'd loved digging her fingers into it and kissing him hard and rough as they'd rolled around his bed. She liked the thickness, and how there was so much to tug and hold on to. She'd even tasted it when he'd covered her with his compact, muscular body and brought her to orgasm.

"Same here," she said.

He laughed. "You like my hair?"

She nodded, digging her fingers into his scalp, further mussing the dark blond cloud of hair. He grinned before sudden concern changed his expression. His crescent-shaped eyes grew wide.

"Damn. Robbie! I'd better go check on him."

He jumped out of bed and pulled on his jeans but not before she enjoyed the view of his sinewy back and handsome behind. He had an obvious tan line left over from summer from surfer-styled trunks.

While he was gone, she stared at the high, beamed ceiling and thought how romantic his French country-style bedroom was. The man had had impeccable taste when it had come to choosing this house. There had to be more to him than met the thoroughly satisfied eye.

He'd also made her feel like a complete woman again. Wow. She stretched and arched in the comfy bed, senses still heightened, enjoying the finely woven sheets against her back. She could get used to this kind of escape. And wasn't that what this two-month job was? An escape from all things?

Phil returned, his smile wide, sexy. "He's still asleep." He stripped and jumped back under the covers with her. "Now, where did we leave off?" He nuzzled her neck and ran a cool hand across her breast. Even if she tried, she couldn't stop her response.

The deliciously warm current he'd started with

his fingertips rolled right to her center and, as quickly as that, she was ready for him again.

Robbie's nap ended much too soon, if you asked Phil. He'd have liked to spend the rest of the night making sexy memories with Stephanie on the best Thanksgiving of his life. But Robbie was awake and protesting by banging on his bedroom door.

"Pill! Whar you?"

"Hang on, Robbie, I'll be right there."

"Don't let him see me in here," Stephanie whispered.

"Okay." He took one last glance at her creamy skin and, yep, her nipples were the same color as her freckles, except, thanks to his attentions, everything about her was much rosier now. He'd have to make a mental snapshot because he had a kid banging on the door.

He hopped into his jeans and strode toward the door, then opened it just enough to squeeze through. "What's up, little dude?"

"I'm hungwee."

"Again?" Phil ruffled Robbie's already messy hair and led him to the kitchen. He smiled at how the boy had put his glasses on lopsided, and how his round belly pushed against the sleeper. The kid was a total wreck, but still managed to look cute.

Did I just use cute in a sentence?

He cut up a piece of pumpkin pie, poured him a glass of milk, and sat him at the kid-size plastic table Roma had left. When he was sure Robbie was preoccupied enough with eating, he slipped back down the hall to check on Stephanie's progress.

She'd put her underwear back on, and the sight of her long torso and shapely legs gave him another pang of pure desire. He couldn't wait to unload Robbie back on Roma and his father. If all went well, they'd arrive home tomorrow, and his bachelor life would finally be back to normal.

"Here you go," he said, handing her the clothes he'd found across the room.

"Thanks."

There was still fire in those dilated pupils, and

it took a lot of restraint to keep from grabbing her and throwing her on the bed again. If he was lucky, he'd have six more weeks of great sex with Stephanie—a gift he hadn't expected when they'd hired the locum.

He liked her pumpkin-colored top just fine, but it looked so much better discarded on the floor. And would he ever take those great legs for granted? Not in six weeks, he wouldn't.

Usually, once he'd been with a woman, he was fine with sending her home, preferring his alone time. But he wasn't anywhere near ready to say goodnight to Stephanie. And he still had Robbie to deal with.

"Can you stick around for another glass of wine or some coffee?"

"You know, I've scheduled that colposcopy for early tomorrow morning," she said, clasping the belt over her hips.

He was fascinated watching her, as if he'd never seen a woman dress before. "Then on Saturday night I want to take you to dinner."

She finished zipping her ankle boots, rushed

him, and brushed his lips with a moist kiss. "I'd like that."

The simple gesture set off another distracting wave of desire. O-*kay*. They had a great thing going, with no strings attached, and as far as he could tell, they were on the same page.

Stephanie willed all the crazy thoughts about the huge mistake she'd made out of her head. By the time her sex-with-Phil high had subsided this morning, she'd realized her blunder. She'd given herself a pep talk on the drive in to the clinic on Friday. Last night had been a one-time thing. She'd gotten carried away, that's all. Phil probably felt obligated to take her out to dinner. For her part, she'd blame it on that evil sweet-tasting red wine she'd imbibed and the sexy wonders of Phil. Heck, she'd already accepted his invitation for dinner on the weekend and, considering his allure, it would be extra-hard to tell him there wouldn't be a repeat bedroom performance.

Old habits were hard to break, and there was

comfort in safety. Why couldn't she figure out what to do?

Celeste Conroy lay on the examination table, prepared for the special procedure. As she'd done countless times before, Stephanie used the colposcope to examine the area of cervix in question and to take a small biopsy.

It only took five minutes.

"You may feel some cramping today. Take it easy. No lifting or straining for a couple of days, and no sex for a week."

The mention of sex sent her mind back to last night with Phil, making her ears burn. She shook her head, hoping to stop the X-rated visions on the verge of materializing in her mind as she made her last few notations on the patient chart.

Celeste, as always, had a slew of questions, and Stephanie was grateful for the distraction.

"I'll need a week to get the results," Stephanie answered, "and I'll call the minute I get them."

The busy morning postponed her curiosity, but by lunchtime, when she still hadn't seen Phil, she asked Gaby.

"He's at the airport, picking up his parents."

He'd made it clear he wanted to take their acquaintance to a whole new level once his parents took Robbie off his hands. The thought made her insides scramble up with anxiety yet excited her at the same time. Soon an unsettled feeling had her finding the nearest mirror and taking a good long look.

Make up your mind, Bennett. Either go for a fling or keep your distance. Don't leave it up to Phil to decide.

Hadn't she given herself permission to let go last night? And hadn't the results been beyond any fantasy she could have dreamed up? After a long inhalation, a tiny smile curved her lips. She had six more weeks in Santa Barbara before she'd be back in her world—why not totally escape from all things Stephanie? And, besides, she'd had her tubes tied—there was nothing to worry about.

The thought of pursuing a carefree romance with Phil launched a wave of flittering wings in her stomach. Did she have the guts to carry it out?

* * *

Well, if this didn't take the prize. If Phil hadn't been so worried about his dad he'd be frustrated by having to hold on to Robbie for a couple more days. The layover at the airport had made Carl sick and Roma had taken him directly to the hospital once they'd landed. He'd picked up a nasty bug and was already showing signs of dehydration. The big iron man Phil had grown up admiring looked far too human in the hospital bed, and it sent a weary wave of dread down his spine.

"I'll keep Robbie for the weekend or until you feel ready to take over," Phil said to Roma.

She sat at her husband's bedside, her dark hair heavily streaked with silver, holding his hand. "If you could bring Robbie by later today, I'd really appreciate it. I miss him so much."

"Go, Roma. You don't have to sit here watching me sleep," Carl said. "Go and see Robbie."

She gave Phil a questioning gaze. How different Roma was from his mother, who'd left when things got tough. His mother's action had jaded Phil and had planted a lifelong mistrust of women. They couldn't be counted on to stick around, so why get serious? Roma broke the mold, but she was the exception.

"Come with me," he said. "Robbie can't wait to see you. I'll drop you back here on my way home."

It dawned on Phil that his fabulous weekend plans, with the hottest lady he'd met in forever, would get put on hold. Again.

Once he sorted things out with Roma and Robbie, he'd give Stephanie a call to give her a heads-up. Either she'd be willing to let Robbie tag along for dinner or they'd take a rain check, but there was no way he'd leave Robbie with a babysitter. The kid would be disappointed enough knowing his mom was back in town yet he still couldn't go home.

How did you explain such a thing to a kid? He'd step back and let Roma do the chore, see how a pro handled it, and maybe learn something.

Later, after he'd heard the latest doctor's report on his father and Robbie was preoccupied with building blocks and making his version of the world's tallest building, or so he'd announced with extra esses and saliva, Phil thought about Stephanie. He thought about how much he'd enjoyed spending Thanksgiving with her, and especially how great it had been to make love to her. And he thought how he'd like to do it again. Soon. But he had to look after the squirt.

So why was there a smile on his face? Because the kid really was a great source of entertainment.

After several attempts, Robbie had made it to ten blocks high, but he'd jumped up and down, knocking the top block off again. Phil stifled a laugh when he glimpsed the expression of frustration cross the boy's face. Phil had to hand it to him, the kid didn't quit. He picked up the same block and balanced it on top of the others, then went hunting for several more.

Phil took the opportunity to call Stephanie. Hearing her soft voice on the phone, it occurred to him how much he'd missed seeing her today, and just how disappointed he was about canceling their plans.

"Looks like I'll be keeping the kid brother for

the weekend," he said on a resigned sigh. Though she'd made real progress being around Robbie on Thanksgiving, he wanted her all to himself the first time he took her out to dinner.

Phil felt compelled to give her the whole story about his father's illness, flight home, and current status. Once he'd filled her in they'd settled into an easy conversation, and as Robbie was still erecting the west-coast version of the Empire State building, he kept talking.

Hell, he'd had sex with the woman. They knew each other intimately now. And though completely out of character, he wanted to take the opportunity to get to know her even better.

"Do you have a minute to talk?" he asked. How busy could a person be in a hotel room?

"Sure," she said.

The problem was that, if he wanted to learn more about her, he'd have to talk about himself. Should he take the risk?

He glanced at Robbie, who'd now moved on to scribbling with crayons in his newest coloring book from Hawaii, and decided what the heck.

"It's been bugging me. I mean, how does a doctor with an aversion to kids wind up being an obstetrician?"

To her credit, she blurted out a laugh instead of taking offense. Though maybe she sounded a little nervous? "I guess it does seem odd, and please don't get me wrong, I love delivering babies. It's just…well, pregnancy and delivery is one thing, and child rearing is another."

"See, now, that's where I get tripped up," Phil said, trying hard to understand her elusive explanation. "It's been my experience that people usually go into a specialty profession because it's their passion. For instance, I chose medicine because of my mother."

Maybe it was the fact that his dad was sick and in a hospital, looking all too frail. Maybe it was because, even after professing to hate his mother all these years, he still missed her, but she'd been on his mind today.

"Your mother wanted you to become a pulmonologist?"

"Actually, she never knew, because I stopped talking to her."

Phil wasn't ready to tell Stephanie the whole story, that he'd been in Australia at a surfing championship when his father had been diagnosed with lymphoma the first time—and that his mother's leaving turned his life upside down. It had made him quit the surfing circuit at twenty to care for his dad and, eventually, head back to school.

"I'm so sorry to hear that, Phil."

He'd confused her. He sensed honest compassion in Stephanie's voice and it felt like a forgiving breath; made him want to be honest with her. Maybe he did owe her an explanation.

"My dad had lymphoma, and when he first got diagnosed, my mother walked out on us. She couldn't deal with his disease. Evidently she didn't give a damn about me either because I never got to say goodbye."

"Oh, God, how awful."

Phil hadn't meant to turn their conversation in this maudlin direction, he'd just wanted to keep her on the phone a little longer, but here he was stripping down barriers and letting the new girl on the block know about the secret of his mother. He could count back ten girlfriends and know for sure they'd never had a clue about his family or whether either of his parents was alive or dead. So why had he opened up to Stephanie?

"Yeah, I haven't talked to her since. I don't have a clue if she knows I'm a doctor or not."

"I see." She sounded suddenly distant.

As he'd gone completely out of character, he decided to get something else off his chest.

"Stephanie, this is a really weird question, but something I noticed yesterday made me wonder if you have a child." The way she'd put Robbie into his pajamas and had left the bedroom door ajar. A novice like himself wouldn't know to do that without being told. But not Stephanie.

She inhaled sharply.

He kicked himself for bringing up the subject. "Are you okay?"

"Yes. Sorry. You caught me off guard, that's all."

He sighed. "Didn't mean to," he said, regretting having mentioned it.

She swallowed. "You and I have something in common."

"How so?"

"You never got to say goodbye to your mother, and I never got to say goodbye to my son."

"Stephanie…" In that moment, he wanted to put down the phone, to crawl inside, and come out the other end. He wanted nothing more than to console her. She had lost a child. "I'm sorry if I—"

"That's okay, Phil. I need to get off the phone now anyway. I'll see you at work," she said, not giving him a chance to say another word.

Confused, he scrubbed his face. All he wanted was an uncomplicated romance, but having lived thirty-five years and dated for twenty of them, he knew there was no such thing.

When Stephanie arrived at work on Monday morning, all the nurses were abuzz with news about the yacht decorations. Gaby had used the office petty cash to purchase six small fake Christmas trees. "They all came complete with lights!" she said animatedly. "Now all we have to do is anchor them on the yacht."

"Great!" Amy said. "And I found my grand-mother's decorations from the old country, and my lederhosen still fit!"

Another nurse chimed in. "I've got a bunch of Philippine Christmas lanterns we can use for one of the trees, too."

Stephanie did her usual fading into the wood-work rather than join in.

Claire appeared, honey-blonde hair pulled back into a long swishy ponytail and green eyes bright with excitement. "Sounds great, guys. Bring ev-erything this Saturday for the decorating party." She saw Stephanie and waved her over. "You're coming, right?"

Stephanie had been keeping a safe distance from the clinic employees. Why get too involved when she was only going to be around for a couple of months? What was the point? Up until this moment she'd planned to blow off the Christmas yacht party, but how could she say no and not appear to be antisocial?

"Um, sure." And, besides, it would give her a chance to see Phil in a perfectly safe environment, one where she couldn't get swept off her resolve to keep a distance.

"Great! I'll send the directions to your email." Claire glanced at her watch and strode for the stairs to her second-floor office. "Talk later."

Well, hell, she'd already had sex with Phil, why not get to know everyone else a little better, too?

The nurses continued to rabbit on about decorating the yacht and what fun it always was as Stephanie smiled and made her way toward her office. After spending an ultra-quiet weekend, she had to admit that she enjoyed the hustle and bustle of the clinic, and with the official invitation now she looked forward to the plans for the coming weekend.

When later that morning Phil loomed in her doorway, her gut clenched. It was the first time she'd seen him since they'd made love. Her heart stumbled over the next couple of beats. He looked amazing with his hair freshly washed and combed straight back. She'd come to notice that however it fell, it stayed, and it always looked great. He'd probably expect further explanation about her weird reaction on the phone on Friday night. She wasn't ready to give it.

"Hey," he said, obviously waiting to be invited in.

"Hi. What's up?" Did her face give her hopeful thoughts away? Was he here to invite her out to lunch or, better yet, a quiet dinner with just the two of them—like the one she'd so looked forward to last weekend? If he did, she hoped he'd keep all conversation superficial.

He carried a large specialty coffee drink in each hand and placed one on her desk. "It's a pumpkin latte. Thought you might like it."

"Thanks." Why did the thoughtful gesture touch her so? Why did it feel so intimate? Before she'd gotten strange on the phone the other night, they'd embarked on a new line of communication. The man had opened up about his mother and because she'd been thinking about Justin after being around Robbie, she'd gone overboard with her response. It must have seemed so strange and out of the blue that she wouldn't have been surprised if he'd avoided her, yet here he was bringing her a drink.

He sat on the edge of her desk and studied her. If the morning sun was brighter than she'd ever seen it, and there wasn't a cloud on the horizon, that's what she imagined the color would be, and it was right there in his eyes.

"So Robbie's going to stay with me the rest of this week, until my dad gets discharged from the hospital." He sounded worn out, like he'd had a super-hard weekend.

As she gazed at him, grateful he hadn't probed more about her son, she caught the telltale signs of sleep deprivation. It looked as if ashes had been faintly smudged beneath his eyes, and his voice sounded huskier than usual. Watching his brother had taken its toll, but Phil wasn't complaining. For a guy who professed to keep things easy and uncomplicated, he'd proved to be deeper than that. And though she wasn't in the market for anything permanent with Phil, this side of his character helped her trust him.

Before he left, he bent over and dropped a sweet kiss on her lips. The simple gesture invited chills. He tasted like pumpkin latte, and after he'd left, she enjoyed sipping her drink and thinking of Phil's kisses for the rest of the afternoon.

Phil had finally gotten Robbie down for the night. All he wanted to do was talk to Stephanie. She'd lost a child and was trying to put her life together. She could use a friend at a time like this, yet she'd chosen to leave the desert during the holidays and spend Christmas with strangers in Santa Barbara.

The last thing he could call himself was a stranger to her, not after their intense lovemaking session the other night. The crazy thing was, it wasn't just about sex with Stephanie. He genuinely liked her. So why not call her, just to talk? The thought made him smile. It reminded him of how in high school he used to have to work up an excuse to call a girl when he liked her. But that had been back in a time of innocence, back when his heart had been eager to fall in love, back when he'd still trusted the opposite sex…back before his mother had walked out.

Yikes, he'd put himself into a lousy mood, and now he needed to call Stephanie to cheer himself up. So that made two reasons, more than enough to make the call.

Robbie came running down the hall in his pajamas. Before Phil had put him to bed, Robbie had talked to his mother and had cried a little. It almost broke Phil's heart. The kid had to settle for second best with him when all he wanted was to sleep in his own bed and get a good-night kiss from his parents. Carl was still in recovery mode, and Roma had her hands full. If Robbie went home too soon, he might feel neglected, and get his feelings hurt.

"I thought I already put you to bed," he said.

"Furgot sumtin'." Robbie used his short, pudgy arms to pull Phil close and tell him, "Wuv you."

Without thinking, Phil kissed him on the fore-head. "Back at ya, little dude. Now, skedaddle back to bed."

Robbie giggled and ran off.

A scary feeling crept over Phil. It had felt nice to kiss his kid brother and, yep, he'd miss him when he was gone.

He stroked his jaw. Maybe he should get a dog.

All the cozy feelings and thoughts about having another warm, living, breathing body share his house boggled his mind. It gave him a third excuse for calling Stephanie—distraction!

"Hey, what's up?" he said, when she answered after the second ring.

"Hi!" Her welcoming tone pushed all his worries aside. All he wanted to do was talk about her day.

After chatting superficially for a while, he realized the real point of his call. He wanted more one-on-one time with Stephanie. Just before hanging up, he said, "And tomorrow lunch is on me."

She answered without hesitation. "Okay. If the weather's nice, maybe we can eat outside."

If he could conjure up warm weather and sunshine for tomorrow he would, but he already felt the equivalent of a sunny day right there—he rubbed the spot—in his chest. "Sounds like a plan."

The next day, though the sky was blue, temperatures were low. Phil and Stephanie wore jackets and set off for the shore anyway. He'd ordered a hearty fish chowder and sourdough rolls from the best deli in town, and carried it in a warming bag with one hand. He longed to place his other arm around her waist but, not wanting to put any pressure on her, he withstood the urge.

He hadn't figured out yet where they stood. The other night he'd been positive she was interested in a no-strings fling for the duration of her stay in Santa Barbara. Since that night—the hottest night he could remember—Stephanie had partially rebuilt that invisible barrier. He knew it had something to do with that weird comment she'd made about not getting to say goodbye to her baby.

He shook his head. The day was too beautiful to try to figure things out. And since when did he get all caught up in really "knowing" a woman? All he knew was that right now the sun danced off the golden highlights in Stephanie's hair, making it look like a shiny copper penny. She smiled whenever she looked at him, and if he didn't get pushy about it, he might just get another kiss before they headed back to the clinic.

They found a bench along the bike path with a shoreline view and sat. She squinted from the bright sun and had to slip on her sunglasses, covering those gorgeous caramel-candy eyes. He was glad to see the smile never left her face.

The simple fact they had time alone together had sparks flying and itchy messages flowing through the circuit board of his body. He'd much rather strip her naked than hand her a cup of soup, but he kept his true desire at bay, and when she took the first taste he received a smile of orgasmic proportions, and that smile was definitely worth his efforts.

Stephanie wasn't very talkative today, but that was okay. He was happy to be with her. Just before he finished dunking the edge of his roll into the last of his soup, his cell phone rang. It was Roma.

"They're going to discharge your dad this afternoon, so I won't be able to pick up Robbie."

"I'll make arrangements," Phil said, realizing he'd gotten pretty blasé about carpools and favors and paybacks with the other mothers from the preschool. They all seemed to really get a kick out of the "cool" surrogate dad on campus. Normally, he would have played the distinction to the hilt. He'd flirt, use them for all the favors they could offer, and maybe even find out if any of the moms were single. But out of respect for his kid brother, he'd done the right thing by taking care of him and hadn't abused the special circumstances.

And, besides, he'd been completely preoccupied with Stephanie.

"Do you want me to keep him tonight, so you and Dad can get settled?"

"That would be wonderful," she said, after an obvious sigh of relief.

Stephanie looked at him as if he were a super-hero or something. In that moment he admitted it: he might just miss the kid once he went home. Maybe…just a little.

He flipped through his contacts on the phone and made a quick call. "Hey, Claire, can you do me a huge favor and pick up Robbie today when you get Gina?" After almost two weeks, he finally understood the bartering side of child care. "Thanks, and I'll drop her off at your house from day care after I get off work."

Stephanie's arms flew around his neck and she planted a cold kiss on his cheek. It wasn't the sexy kind of kiss he'd been hoping for, but he wouldn't complain. He turned the angle of his face so their lips could meet, and dropped a peck on her mouth. This was all way too affectionate for his taste. He preferred sexy and hot, but the weirdest thing was, he kind of liked it.

"I guess we better be getting back to the clinic," he said. "Looks like Robbie and I are roommates for one more night."

CHAPTER SEVEN

THURSDAY morning lab results planted a rock-size knot firmly into Stephanie's stomach. Celeste Conroy's biopsy showed squamous cell carcinoma. After last Thursday and Thanksgiving, Maria was back today, sitting on the other side of Stephanie's desk, waiting expectantly for the day's assignment.

"Well," Stephanie said, handing the printed pathology report to the RNP student. "This is a perfect example of what makes this job a challenge."

"Wow," Maria said. "She's pregnant, right? How do you handle something like this?"

"I tell her the truth. We need to find out how extensive the cancer is and I'll need to do a conization of her cervix."

She'd remove a thick cone-shaped wedge of tissue from the area in question of the cervix, extending high into the cervical canal. Her goal would be to leave a wide margin of normal cells around the area of cancer.

"Risks?" Maria queried.

"Yes, but we must always balance them against the benefits. I'll do everything in my power to keep both the mother and the baby healthy." Stephanie glanced over her calendar for the earliest possible appointment. "I want to do the biopsy on Monday so I can get this mother-to-be some good news before Christmas." She shuddered, thinking of all the potential possibilities, and willed a positive attitude.

"Would it be okay if I came in to observe?" Maria patted her protruding pregnancy as worry lines etched her brow.

"Of course."

Stephanie's pulse had worked its way into her mouth. She punched in the phone number, willing her quivery hand to settle down, then cleared her throat. She needed to sound confident when she gave the diagnosis, for the patient's sake.

* * *

Stephanie couldn't believe the choreographed chaos on Saturday morning at the harbor. Even halfway down the harbor she could hear lively Christmas music over the loudspeaker. The pungent sea air seemed to heighten her senses, making her feel alive and excited. She stopped in midstep, having never seen a more gorgeous boat. As promised, everyone from the clinic had showed up with their contribution. She'd even made an extra effort to buy several strings of Christmas lights for the yacht.

Jason greeted her with a captain's smile and waved her aboard. Before she boarded, she noticed the name on the bow— *For Claire*. Something about that special touch pinched at her heart. She'd heard bits and pieces about Claire and Jason's love affair. It hadn't been easy for either of them to admit they'd fallen in love, yet now they made a perfect couple. She shook her head. Why were people so slow to figure things like that out?

"This is my latest indulgence," Jason said, grinning and patting the rail. "I wanted to upgrade, anyway."

Claire, wearing a teal-colored windbreaker and matching ball cap, with her long ponytail sticking out the hole in the back, stood at his side, smiling up at him. "He made sure there were plenty of shady spots when he designed this boat, because of my lupus. Come on, I'll show you around."

Amy and Gaby worked diligently on placing the small Christmas trees at key positions on the bow, stern, port, and starboard. Other nurses and aides helped stabilize and decorate them. They waved hello, and the simple greeting made Stephanie feel like part of the clinic family. Maybe it would have happened sooner if she'd reached out to them. Well, better late than never.

Just when Claire was about to take Stephanie below deck, she saw Phil rushing down the dock with a huge pink box in his arms. He waved at her and smiled, and her insides got jumbled up. Jason met him dockside and shook his hand.

"I brought doughnuts," Phil said.

"Yay," Amy said, as Gaby applauded.

"I'm making cocoa," Claire called over her shoulder, leading Stephanie by the arm down to the galley. Stephanie was grateful for the distraction to buy time to straighten out her suddenly fuzzy thoughts.

Wow. Stephanie had never seen a more modern galley on a boat. Granted, her experience with boats was woefully limited, but still. Stainless-steel appliances, perfectly stained woodwork and cupboards; the compact galley oozed class.

As Claire stirred a huge pot of milk, adding cocoa liberally, she seemed her usual self from work, but more relaxed and completely carefree. "I'd never been on a sailboat until I met Jason. Now I'm ready to give up my practice, home-school Gina, and sail around the world with him." A soft laugh gently bubbled out. "Don't worry, we won't quit our day jobs. Too many people need us at that clinic, and I love it there. But maybe someday…"

"You must take some great weekend getaways," Stephanie said, gathering the red paper cups decorated with wreaths and garland trim and placing them on a large tray.

"Not as often as we'd like, but we have plans for a longer trip this summer. Thought we'd sail up to San Francisco and back."

"Wow," Stephanie said. "That's impressive." She held the tray close so Claire could ladle out the cocoa into the cups then she shook the whipped cream can and sprayed a dollop on top of each.

"If all goes well, maybe the year after we'll set sail for Hawaii."

"Sounds like a dream come true."

Before she could say more, a familiar bedroom-sexy voice vibrated from the doorway into the main saloon. "You ladies need a hand?" Phil hung in the doorway, opening up his broad chest, cutting a V down to a trim waist. Her throat went dry, so strong was her reaction, and she suddenly needed a sip of cocoa. "I think we've got this covered."

She did her best to act casual, as if the mere presence of the man didn't scatter her nerves.

He jabbed a thumb over his shoulder. "The folks

have already eaten most of the doughnuts, but I saved you ladies a couple."

"Thanks. We'll be right up," Claire said, oblivious to the caveman-sexy gaze streaming from Phil's sea-blue eyes and directed at Stephanie.

How in the world would she make it through the day without mauling the man?

She'd been losing sleep, having hot and restless dreams of tussling in bedsheets with a strange man. The dreams had been so realistic; she could practically feel the man's weight on her body, driving himself into her. Hell, she knew exactly who the guy was. Phil. One time she'd woken up with the covers on the floor, throbbing thighs, sheets wadded in her fists, panting, and *very* frustrated. How in the world should she handle her desire where Phil was concerned?

They were both adults—why not enjoy each other?

Later, as she and Phil put the finishing touches on the mainsail Christmas lights, she jumped at his touch.

"Sorry," she said, as electricity powered through her veins.

"You seem a bit flinchy," he said, drilling her with a stare.

"I'm just a little uptight with all the new patients and work and all."

Phil lowered his voice and lifted her hair, hooking it behind one ear. "It's Christmastime, pretty baby, loosen up." The raucous version of *Rockin' Around the Christmas Tree* nearly drowned out his words. "You know, a little TLC might be just the thing you need."

A vision of tender loving care, compliments of Phil, whirled through her mind. She couldn't breathe for a second. He'd spoken the words she'd been afraid to acknowledge. He seemed to know exactly what she'd been thinking, and now her cheeks were probably betraying her by blushing hot pink. She glanced around the busy deck. Fortunately, everyone seemed oblivious to them.

Why not? Why the hell not have a fling? Was she such a wretched person that she didn't deserve a little pleasure in life? Phil had already proved what a fantastic lover he was. He hadn't pushed her into doing anything she hadn't wanted to. Hell, she'd come up with all kinds of ideas in her dreams lately. It could be fun to try them out… with Phil.

Did she really want to balance on the precipice of sexual frustration for another month, or slide back into that incredible place he'd taken her before?

How many times did she need to give herself permission to live?

Her cheeks flamed and her palms tingled, thinking about it. Slowly, she glanced into his darkening and decidedly sexy stare.

"Robbie went home last night," he said, eyes never wavering from hers. "And I owe you that dinner out. What about tonight?"

What about tonight? She knew what he meant, what he wanted.

He'd sounded the same when he'd made love to her. Phil's voice, full of intimate intention, massaged her rising senses, snapping to life key areas and a powerful drive to scratch the itch with him.

So strong was her physical reaction that if everything else could just disappear, she'd be on him, knocking him down and ripping off his clothes right this instant.

Nearly trembling with desire, she found her voice, if only a whisper. "Yes. Tonight."

That evening, Stephanie had talked herself down from the frantic sexual cliff, but excitement still washed over every cell in her body. She couldn't wait to see Phil again, to be alone with him. The permission she'd given herself to be with him had been so incredibly freeing.

He picked her up at her hotel looking impeccable. He wore a perfectly tailored sport coat, dark slacks, and a pale blue shirt open at the collar. Did he realize how the color brought out his eyes? His hair, brushed back from his forehead, curled beneath his earlobes. And that smile—did she stand a chance resisting it? She didn't want to!

She'd rushed to the Paseo after they'd finished

decorating the boat that afternoon and bought a little black dress. Now, standing before his scrutinizing eyes, she tugged at the skirt with shaky hands. Maybe tonight's seduction wouldn't be as easy as she'd fantasized. She didn't want her nerves to ruin things.

"Wow," he said. "You look spectacular."

His reaction nearly knocked her off her spiky heels. It was exactly what she'd wanted to hear. He liked what he saw, and that made her ecstatic. In her fantasy, she was a vamp, but here, in front of Phil, all she could say was, "Thanks."

His gaze lingered several moments then he scanned from her hair to her brightly polished toes. As if his head was a glass globe, she could practically see his thoughts. He liked what he saw and wanted to indulge. Just as quickly, he snapped out of the spell.

"I hope you've got a warm coat," he said, brushing a light kiss across her cheek. Man, he smelled as good as he looked. "We'll be eating outside."

What did she care? It would give her an excuse to cuddle up close to him.

They entered the restaurant, called Bouchon, through a shrubbery-hidden portal, and the first thing Stephanie noticed was shiny light wood floors. The decor was understated yet classy, utilizing matching light wood tables and chairs, and cream-colored tablecloths. Huge modern art canvases supplied needed color on the walls. Her first impression was that the total dining effect was as warm and welcoming as Phil's hand pressing against hers.

Phil seemed to know the proprietor of the restaurant and had gotten them a perfectly placed table on the patio. He guided her with his palm at her waist, the barely there pressure at her back already setting off chill rockets. Even though every seat was taken, their cozy corner felt as intimate as Phil's eyes. The brisk evening air mingled with radiant restaurant heat lamps to create the best of both outdoor and indoor worlds.

Stephanie inhaled and rolled her shoulders, inviting the long-overdue relaxation to settle in.

Phil's taste was flawless. The wine crisp from nearby vineyards, appetizers made from local farmers' market ingredients, and the main course free range from Santa Barbara microranches.

Stephanie savored the exquisite taste of plump sea scallops, sharing the appetizer with Phil and with a perfect glass of Chardonnay. He'd insisted she try the seared duck as her main course, the signature dish of the great chef. Who was she to argue?

He took her hand in his and gazed appreciatively into her eyes. "I'm really glad we finally got our date."

So this was what it had all come down to. She hadn't planned on sleeping with him on Thanksgiving, but hadn't regretted it for a second. She'd backtracked a bit from her permission, but seeing Phil as a whole person, committed to his job and connected to his family, drove her to know him more. The decision to take the moment by the horns and ride it for all it was worth, or walk away a frustrated and closed-off woman, remained in her hands.

She glanced at Phil, latticed moonlight shadows

making him all the more intriguing. The decision seemed obvious.

She couldn't help but smile as warm tingles worked their way through her insides. She could blame it on the wine and great food, but she knew better. Only Phil could set that kind of reaction twisting through her. Her decision final, she'd skip dessert at the restaurant, instead saving up for the special delights that Phil Hansen had to offer.

Three hours later, flat on her back, Stephanie lay panting, staring at the ceiling, flushed and tingling…everywhere! Phil should have a doctorate in making love.

Never in her life had she given in to her desires, completely exempt of expectations, and gone with her mood. Until now. With Phil. He had a way of drawing that out of her. She didn't feel tawdry about it, either. With him, making love came as naturally as breathing, and, boy, was she out of breath.

He nuzzled her neck, sending yet another wave

of chills across her skin. "That was perfect," he said, husky and still revved up.

She slipped her arm across his torso and curled into his shoulder. Secure in his embrace, and content beyond words, she sighed. "We'll have to do this again sometime."

His devilish laugh vibrated through his chest. "Why not right now?" He got up on his elbows and looked deep into her eyes. "You're incredible, you know that?"

Did she know that? Had her husband ever told her she was incredible? They'd been in love once upon a time—she'd known that much for sure. When she'd become pregnant, she'd been happier than she'd ever been, but months later things had changed.

Her hand brushed over her abdomen, imagining the fallopian tubes she'd had tied off. She was safe. She'd never get pregnant again.

Phil's mouth pressed gently against her jaw. He glanced into her eyes again, as if he'd seen her secret fleeting thoughts. The next kiss he delivered was warm and caring. The tender gesture nearly split her heart.

She kissed him back, ragged and hard, her fingers digging into that glorious hair. If she was having a fling with Phil, she couldn't allow emotions or any feelings beyond passion and excitement to get in the way.

Sunday, after making her breakfast in bed—Phil had *been* breakfast—he talked her into hitting the beach for a game of volleyball.

She couldn't help but grin at the invitation. Surfing may be his turf, but volleyball was definitely hers. After a few warm-up shots, they *thwopped* the ball back and forth across the net. Her toes dug into the sand, the fresh sea breeze making her skin feel as vibrant and warm as Phil's touch had the night before, as warm as the sun heating her scalp and shoulders. Phil popped a ball off his fingertips, and out of reflex she spiked it over the net, hitting him smack between the eyes. Shock quaked through her body as she rushed to him.

He rubbed his nose, looking dazed. "Great shot, Bennett!"

After she made sure he was okay, the surprised look on his face set her off laughing. She crumpled to her knees, overcome with the giggles.

He swooped her up into his arms and ran toward the water. Weak with laughter, she didn't protest, until he ran knee-deep into a wave and tossed her into the chilly ocean. Her scream was cut short by salt water. Once she regained her bearings, she chased Phil toward the beach and made a poor excuse for a tackle, only managing to grab his ankles and falling flat.

This carefree feeling felt as foreign as having that ocean, crashing and constant, in Palm Desert. She welcomed the new sensation, breathing deeper and feeling more vital than she had in years.

He broke away from her grasp and sat back on his ankles, grinning. His high-pitched laugh and corny smile egged her on. She crawled toward him and threw her arms around his neck then planted a wet and salty kiss on his mouth. Though

clumsy at first, the kiss soon turned passionate, his hands wandering, holding her as if he
never wanted to let go. With their lips smashing
and tongues mingling, she thought how close to
heaven it felt being here on the beach with Phil.
How he managed to wipe away her worries with
a single heart-stopping kiss.

As they rolled around, their kisses became in-
vaded by sand, and soon her sexy moment turned
to awareness that every crease and crevice of her
body was sticky with beach grit. And after he'd
made the same discovery, they lay side by side,
flat on their backs, laughing together.

It seemed the playboy of Santa Barbara had
resuscitated her life. Yeah, to use his own
words, their fling *was* just what the doctor had
ordered.

After he'd taken her to the hotel to shower and
clean up, they went to lunch at the yacht club.
During a long walk along the seashore, Phil invited her to his house again. The memory of being
lost in his body, oblivious to her thoughts, lured
her back to his bed.

Though anything but rehearsed, their lovemaking became more familiar. They'd explored each other's bodies with abandon, and she'd delighted in discovering his sensitive spots. She loved the texture of his skin, so many shades darker than her own. The ease with which he responded to her touch made her smile. She felt as though she could weave magic with him, especially when he was deep inside her, expertly guiding her to her final release.

Sex with Phil was nothing short of enchanting, and she hoped to stay under the spell for as long as she stayed in Santa Barbara.

Once completely sated, she flopped limply on top of him, and lifted her hair from her hot and sticky shoulders.

He blew lightly on her neck. "Stay with me tonight."

Reality checked back in. "I can't. I've got to be well rested for the conization tomorrow morning."

"Come back tomorrow night, then," he mur-

mured, his hand playing with tendrils of her hair.

"I thought you were a love-'em-and leave-'em kind of guy?" Her true thought about his reputation had tumbled out before she could censure it.

In one quick move, he grabbed her and flopped her onto her back. Settling himself between her thighs, he gazed confidently into her face. "I'm just getting started with you."

It wasn't the most romantic thing she'd ever heard, yet, as he nibbled her earlobe, it thrilled her just the same. He hadn't grown tired of her yet, and, heaven knew, she wasn't even close to getting bored with him. Couldn't imagine it. Yet she wasn't as easily lured into his spell this time. Her mind wandered.

As life and her job wedged into her thoughts, she switched to the practical side of her life, and pragmatic words followed. "How does it work with you? How do you know when it's time to move on?"

The leftover fairy dust from their heated sex vanished.

He rolled onto his back and stared at the ceiling. "Where'd that come from?"

"I'm curious. That's all."

He rose up onto one elbow. "I'm not nearly as callous as my reputation."

"I didn't call you callous. All I did was ask how you know when a 'fling' is over."

He took her hand and kissed her fingers, cleverly diverting her attention. "Let's just say I'm nowhere near that with you."

The perfect answer from a master. He was a playboy after all, and she couldn't forget it.

Stephanie saw so much potential with Phil, yet he seemed a man of contradictions. Regardless of his stereotypical-playboy dating pattern, he lived in a house perfect for a family. He liked to dawdle in the kitchen, and garden! And when push came to shove about looking after his kid brother, he'd proved himself worthy. Phil was full of potential. Not that she was looking for anyone. No. Not that he'd ever consider her for more than a few nights of great sex.

She glanced at him, as if seeing for the first time the truth of their bond. They had nowhere to go but here, his bed. She was thankful for him forcing her out of her shell, but reality had a mean spirit and it had just smacked her in the face.

Phil took her hand and kissed her fingertips.

How long would she be able to overlook his playboy ways? Would it tear her heart out when he lost interest and moved on? Would he have the courtesy to wait until she'd moved back to Palm Desert? He'd been evasive when she'd questioned him.

She glanced into his unwavering eyes. He smiled at her, but she couldn't return it, wondering instead if anyone would ever be able to tame him. These were not the thoughts of a woman having a fling. She shouldn't be concerned with them. Yet she was.

She fought off a wave of regret, refusing to let it blemish their fantastic weekend. Then with a sudden need to retreat back to her protective shell, to hide behind the medical profession, she kissed his forehead.

"I've got a big day tomorrow." With nothing further to say, she slipped out from under the sheets, gathered her clothes strewn across the floor and bedroom love seat, and padded toward the bathroom.

"I'll let myself out," she said.

CHAPTER EIGHT

PHIL rubbed his temples and squinted. What in the hell had just happened? He and Stephanie had had great sex over the weekend, he'd enjoyed every minute he'd spent with her, then whammo! She'd slipped back into stranger mode.

He sat at the bedside and gulped down a glass of water. His head pounded behind his temples. Sex was supposed to release endorphins, and they were supposed to make a guy feel great. And they had…until she'd withdrawn.

He thought of Stephanie wrapped in his arms one minute and gone the next. He wasn't sure what he wanted with her beyond what they already had—great fun, great sex, good times—but then what? She'd leave for the desert.

Buck naked, he paced the length of his bedroom. Give her a day to herself. Bring her lunch.

Invite her for Chinese food after work another night. No pressure. He'd do what he did best— charm the hell out of a woman.

And though it would be hard, he'd keep his hands to himself, because he didn't want to lose what little ground he'd gained with her.

The Christmas lights parade was on Saturday, and he hoped she'd be there. If the magic of Christmas couldn't break down the last of her barriers, nothing would.

He stopped in midpace and stared at his feet. Stephanie had given him the perfect opportunity to let another relationship slip away. Letting a woman loose had never bothered him. Over the years he'd learned new and creative ways to let his lady friends down gently. He'd buy them an expensive bracelet or necklace, tell them they deserved so much better than him. Yeah, he'd even stooped so low as to use his "busy career" as an excuse. And if he saw that special twinkle in the lady's eyes, he'd announce that he never wanted to be a father, even though in reality his own father meant the world to him.

There were always other women out there. But this time around he wanted Stephanie. Hell, he liked her. A lot. He thought about her lilting laugh when they playfully wrestled on his bed. Up close and personal, those tiny freckles bridging her nose turned him on more than he cared to admit. And her skin. Damn, she felt like velvet under his gardener's calluses. And she was a fantastic doctor. Everyone at the clinic had commented, now that she'd started mixing with them, on how well she fit in. Truth was, he liked the whole Stephanie Bennett package.

Complete silence echoed off the walls and drowned out his thoughts. He had to admit that at times like this he missed the thudding of Robbie's pudgy feet, and he definitely missed Stephanie Bennett in his bed.

Was this foreign feeling loneliness?

Maybe it was time to get a dog. In the meantime, he'd see if a football game was on TV.

On Monday morning, Christmas music streamed through the office speakers, grabbing Stephanie's attention. Gaby had obviously been busy decorating over the weekend. Maybe the boat-decorating party had put her in the mood. She'd set up a miniature Christmas village behind the reception window, complete with mock snow and twinkling lights. Wreaths hung at each doctor's door, and a banner wishing everyone a happy holiday was draped across the entryway to the waiting room.

The cheery atmosphere seemed contrary to what Stephanie had scheduled first thing that morning in the clinic. She got settled in her office and did a quick mental rundown of how the procedure would be carried out then noticed Maria standing expectantly in her doorway. She welcomed her in—having Maria as moral support was nice.

"I'm planning on doing a cold-knife conization. It may produce more bleeding than other procedures, but it doesn't obscure the surgical margins as much as the two other techniques, which is very important."

Stephanie drew a diagram for Maria. "While were there, I'm going to go ahead and perform

a cerclage to minimize the bleeding and to protect from premature labor down the road." She
sketched as Maria looked on, outlining how
she planned to remove the wedge of tissue then
stitch the cervix together to keep it tight until
delivery.

"Amy is having Celeste sign the consent in the
procedure room. Are you ready?"

Maria nodded, her espresso-brown eyes
wide and intelligent. She tottered beside her
as Stephanie made her way to the special-
procedure room. Even though it seemed impossible for Maria's pregnant belly to look any bigger,
it did, and Stephanie wondered how she could
possibly hold out until her due date.

Stephanie greeted Celeste Conroy with a firm
handshake as the patient reclined on the table
with a paper shield across her lap and her feet in
place in the stirrups. Amy had already set her up
for the cervical cone biopsy.

"You remember Maria Avila, the nurse practitioner student?"

Celeste gave permission for Maria to observe,

and Stephanie was glad of the extra pair of hands.

Amy had given Celeste a mild sedative on her arrival and Stephanie administered a local cervical block. As they waited for it to take effect, Celeste had more questions.

"The consent said a lot of scary things," Celeste said. "Can they all happen?"

"The consents have to list every single possibility. Will they all happen? No. Will any of them happen? Not likely. Please don't let it scare you. The main thing I want to make sure about is the bleeding. Pregnancy increases blood flow to the uterus and cervix, so it might get tricky, but I'll be extra-careful."

"What if we don't get all of the cancer out with this procedure?"

"There is a very low risk that your lesion will progress during the course of your pregnancy. My job is to remove it all today, and I'm confident I can. Let's take this one step at a time."

Reluctantly, Celeste agreed, and as the sedative wove its spell, she plopped her head back on the exam table and stared off into the distance. Stephanie could only imagine the thoughts she must be having.

Once the wedge of tissue was excised and placed in a specimen container, Stephanie used electrocautery to control the rapid local bleeding, then, as planned, performed the cervical cerclage.

"Maria, I'm going to assign you to Recovery. I want to watch Mrs. Conroy for the next four hours. Amy, will her husband be on hand to drive her home later?"

Amy nodded.

Stephanie ran down a long list of things Celeste needed to avoid for the next week, and wrote everything down. Knowing her patient had been sedated, she planned to go over everything again later when her husband was present and ready to take her home.

"Let me know if there's any unusual bleeding," Stephanie said to Maria on her way out.

"Will do."

Stephanie went about the rest of her morning clinic, only occasionally allowing Phil to slip into her thoughts. She wasn't looking for a husband or a future father. She'd gone that route and failed miserably, and had ensured she'd never be a mother again. All she wanted to do was put the pieces of her life back together, and maybe, while she was here, have a little fun. So if he was only a guy to have fun with, why was she thinking about him so much? Maybe it was because he'd turned out to be so great with Robbie. She'd seen him go from clueless to expert in less than two weeks. The guy had father potential written all over him. In a twisted sort of way, after she left, she hoped he'd find a woman who could give him a family one day.

"Dr. Bennett?" Amy interrupted her confusing thoughts. "Maria sent me to tell you that Mrs. Conroy has soaked through several pads already."

Alarm had Stephanie picking up her phone and dialing Jason Rogers's office. He met her at the patient's gurney, as she finished her examination.

"I need to cauterize more extensively, and

then I'd like to admit the patient for overnight observation," she said.

"I'll call the hospital and tell them we're sending her," Jason said.

"I don't have privileges there, so I'll need you to admit her."

"No problem," he said. "Whatever you need."

Having such support and backup from her boss meant the world to her. And after the second round of cauterizing the wedge margins, the cervical bleeding already showed signs of slowing. Still, she couldn't be too careful with her patient, and, more importantly, with the pregnancy.

The transporters arrived, and Maria volunteered to ride over with Celeste so Stephanie could finish her clinic appointments. She'd head over to the hospital as soon as she was finished.

By the end of the day, Stephanie hadn't seen even a glimpse of Phil, and she figured if he was avoiding her she deserved it for pulling back and leaving without a proper goodbye. What did he expect? They really were nothing more than bed partners so she had no obligation to him. Then why did him avoiding her bother her so much? She bit her lip and sighed.

Because she cared about him.

"Is Dr. Bennett in?" Phil asked Gaby on his way into the clinic on Tuesday morning.

"She's at the hospital, discharging one of her patients."

He'd decided to ask her to lunch today, and was eager to see her again. When he got to his office and booted up his computer, a calendar alert popped up at the moment Jon strode through his door.

"You ready?" Jon asked.

Damn, he'd forgotten the symposium in Ventura he and Jon had signed up for months ago to attend together today.

So much for lunch with Stephanie.

On Wednesday, Phil got called into the E.R. for an emergency thoracentesis in the morning, and by the time he'd caught up with his patient load that evening, Stephanie had already left for the day.

He could give her a call and ask her out for dinner, but he knew how easy it was to blow someone off over the phone, so he decided to wait until Thursday morning when he could see her face-to-face.

On Thursday, when there was no sign of Stephanie at the clinic, Phil discovered through Jason that she'd been invited to the local university to speak to Maria's fellow nurse-practitioner students.

Things weren't looking good, and, though contrary to his natural desire to see her as soon as possible, he decided to wait until Saturday evening at the postholiday-parade party at Jason's house. He'd missed her all week, and wanted to iron out that wrinkle in their relationship, the unspoken knowledge about his dating history. He understood how it must look to a woman like Stephanie. He couldn't make any guarantees, of course, but she seemed worth delving deeper into—dared he use the word?—a relationship. He scraped his jaw. It wasn't just any girl he'd ask to help with the task he had planned.

* * *

This is nuts, Stephanie thought as she drove back to her hotel from the university. Maybe the move to Santa Barbara and starting to practice medicine again had been more stressful than she'd expected. Each night this week she'd been dead tired, and the springboard of emotions that getting to know Phil had created couldn't be denied. Maybe she was premenstrual? She rubbed her forehead and mentally did some math. It was December 9 and she was supposed to have started her period on December 2. She'd been like clockwork ever since she'd had her tubes tied. Today she felt a little foggy headed and maybe a little tender in her breasts. She'd probably get her period any day now.

But she was a week late, and hadn't so much as spotted.

She shook her head as she pulled into her parking space at the hotel. It had to be stress.

California had a reputation for perfect weather, and on this Saturday in mid-December, while the rest of the country dealt with snowstorms and arctic cold snaps, the sky was clear and the temperature was in the high sixties. Rain was predicted for early tomorrow morning, but you couldn't prove it by the sky overhead.

Stephanie shaded her eyes with her palm and enjoyed the sight of the setting sun over the glistening blue ocean, then took a deep breath of salty air as she walked down the docks to Jason's berth.

An hour earlier she'd come off the phone from a conversation with Celeste Conroy, who continued to improve since the bleeding scare earlier in the week. The best part of all was being able to tell her they'd successfully removed the small cancerous area on her cervix, and the tissue margins were all clear. If all continued to go well, the cerclage would keep her from going into premature labor later on.

Stephanie decided to compartmentalize her professional and personal life. With her duties as a physician completed today, she removed the mental stethoscope and…oh, hell…prepared to be Santa's helper. Nerves tangled in her stomach at the thought of confronting Phil after walking out on him the other night.

A memo had gone out at work, "Wear your most outrageous Christmas sweater," and she'd made a quick run to the Paseo to find something to fit the theme, but was too embarrassed to put it on until she got there.

Jason's yacht was decked out with the Midcoast Medical employees' handy Christmas decorations, and from this vantage point the boat promised, when lit up later, to thrill the spectators.

She smiled, even as her stomach fought off another wave of nervous flitters. She hadn't seen Phil all week except for fleeting moments coming and going at the clinic. She'd avoided his gaze once, and another time he made an abrupt turn and entered Jon's office. She'd failed miserably as fling material.

Claire waved and greeted her from the deck. An adorable curly-headed child with huge blue eyes stood by her side, and another baby, getting pushed back and forth in a stroller, sat plump and contentedly swaddled in extra blankets.

"This is my daughter, Gina," Claire said, then nodded toward the stroller. "And this is Jason Junior."

Looking more petulant than shy, Gina hugged her mother's thigh and buried her face rather than say hello. Claire smoothed the girl's hair with her free hand.

Stephanie gave herself a quick pep talk about not letting the children make her nervous. They were Claire's children, not hers, and from the look of it, Claire handled the job with aplomb. It was Christmas, a child's favorite time of year, and there was no way Stephanie could avoid missing her son, but just for today she vowed to not let it get her down. Just for today she'd let Christmas joy rub off on her and she'd smile along with everyone else on this festive occasion. Then, on Christmas Day, she would withdraw into her shell with her constant companion of grief.

She boarded the boat, her sweater in the original shopping bag, and almost immediately lost her balance when someone grabbed her knees. She reached for the boat rail and glanced down in time to hear a familiar squeal of hello. "Robbie, what are you doing here?"

"I get to thit on Thanta's knee," he said, pride beaming from his eyes.

"Me, too!" Gina had found her voice and chose to use it to stake her rightful claim.

Robbie made his version of a mean face at Gina—the silly scrunched-up look almost made Stephanie laugh—and crossed his arms. "He my brother."

"This was my bright idea," Claire said, looking apologetic. "Maybe I should have thought this through a little more."

Phil seemed to materialize from thin air. A sudden pop of adrenaline quickened her pulse. She'd pretend, for Claire's sake, that everything was normal.

Phil hadn't noticed her yet, but Jason and Gaby had obviously noticed him, and laughed. He'd gone for Surfer Dude Santa with belly pad beneath a reindeer-patterned Hawaiian shirt and red velvet pants with suspenders. And good sport that he was, he'd stuck an all-in-one Santa hair and beard combo on his head like a helmet. A huge grin made his eyes crinkle at the edges as he modeled his ridiculous outfit. His California version of Santa might raise brows, but it would fit right in with Santa Barbara and was the perfect touch for their Christmas-themed yacht.

He made a slow turn, hands out to allow Jason and Gaby to see the entire costume, including the surfboard-toting reindeer on the shirt. They blurted out a laugh. He'd been hoodwinked into the job and, instead of griping, he'd good-naturedly put his signature on it. The thought tugged at Stephanie's heart, and a bizarre notion catapulted through her brain. She could fall in love with a guy like Phil…if she didn't watch out.

Phil finally noticed her, and she saw a subtle change in his self-mocking. When their eyes met for a brief second, he nodded and her legs turned to water. She nodded back, unsure if she'd be able to talk coherently to him. Gina and Robbie, rushing to greet Santa, put a quick stop to her fears.

"Santa, Santa," the children chanted.

Suddenly distracted, Phil hugged both of them.

An irrational sense of hurt made her fear she'd blown everything by leaving on Sunday night.

"Claire, I tell you, Roma and Dad will do anything for a cheap babysitter and a night out." He gave a good-hearted shrug, as if he was putting on a carefree performance for her sake. "It's a good thing I've got two knees," he said. "Ho, ho, ho."

Though sounding more resigned and not even close to a real Santa impersonator's laugh, he still delighted the kids. And Stephanie thought he might feel as much at a loss as she did about how to handle things between them.

"He's coming to my house first," Gina chided Robbie.

"Nah-uh," Robbie was quick to reply, arms tightly folded over his chest. "Mine."

"Go get dressed," Gaby said from over Stephanie's shoulder. She wore a gaudy red Christmas sweater that clashed with her magenta hair, and nudged Stephanie toward the stairs. "I want to take group pictures before it gets too crowded."

Whisked away to change, Stephanie barely had a moment to think about anything but putting on the Christmas sweater complete with a string of flashing Christmas lights on the appliquéd quilted tree. Aside from her mixed-up feelings about Phil, it actually felt good walking among the living again.

When she went up on deck, Jason had already turned on the lights. Everything twinkled and shone and the sight took her breath away. They really had created a winter wonderland. A dozen colorful strings of lights had been extended from the tip of the mainsail, from where they fanned out and were attached to the deck in a Christmas tree shape. At the top was a huge white lighted star. The half-size internationally decorated trees blinked and blinged, and with the added touch of a Scotsman, a Russian, a cowboy, a Dane and a Filipino standing next to them, they painted an impressive picture. Several lighted wreaths were hung strategically along the boat railing, and pine garland loaded heavily with glittery balls and blinking lights outlined the rails.

To top things off, two huge flashing neon Merry Christmas signs adorned both the bow and the stern. The remaining clinic employees sat on deck, wearing knitted caps and mufflers, assorted loud holiday sweaters and singing Christmas carols. If they didn't win first place in the Santa Barbara Chamber of Commerce Christmas lights parade, they should at least win the gaudiest-boat award!

Swept up with the holiday spirit, Stephanie couldn't help but laugh to herself. She hadn't felt this excited about celebrating Christmas in years, and it felt pretty darn great…until she came face-to-face with Santa.

He looked as uncomfortable as she felt. If only she could think of something witty to say. Something that would break this awkward trance they seemed stuck in.

"Nice sweater," he said, with the hint of teasing in his eyes.

It was the perfect excuse to lighten things up between them, to call a truce, and she grabbed it. "I like your suspenders, too."

They smiled cautiously at each other. His solid bedroom stare cut through her facade and flustered her. She focused on his white cloud of hair and beard for distraction, realizing she'd never think of Santa the same way again.

"Hey, let me get a picture," Jon said, camera in place, ready for his shot.

"Me, too," Gaby chimed in, at his side.

René stood smiling behind Jon, holding a bundle of baby wrapped in half a dozen blankets. "You may as well let them," she said. "They'll just keep pestering you until you pose."

Phil took Stephanie by the arm, pulled her closer, and whispered, "Smile pretty for the camera."

His unflappable charm disarmed her, all the apprehension she'd clung to vanishing. Maybe she was in over her head, but she couldn't deny her attraction to him.

"Great," Jon said. "Now let's go for a group shot."

Jason appeared, decked out in a captain's cap

with minilights that blinked on and off. Everyone else lined up around him.

Almost as if being transported back in time, the magic and mystery of Christmas overcame Stephanie. Her skin became covered with goose bumps and her eyes prickled. It felt too good. She didn't deserve to feel this happy…during the holidays.

"Okay, that's enough," Phil said, clutching her arm and nudging her toward his appointed chair as if sensing her mood change. "We have work to do. How did I get talked into this again?" He stared into her eyes, where tears were threatening. "Oh, right—you!"

"I abstained, remember?" she said, grateful that everything seemed back to normal between them. It helped snap her out of the weepiness.

Deeply grateful for this night and all the distractions, she took her place and waved toward Jon on the docks as he snapped several more group shots. Then Jason backed the vessel out of the berth, laying on the air horn for a long and attention-getting blast.

Claire lifted first Gina and then Robbie onto Phil's lap. He pulled his chin in, as if aliens from planet Xenon had just been dropped from a spacecraft.

"Listen up, you two." Claire held each of their chins in a hand. "Do not get down from Santa's lap. Do you understand?"

Mesmerized by her firm clutch, they gave her their undivided attention and both nodded.

Though more relaxed with Robbie, Phil looked completely out of his element, with Gina bouncing excitedly on his knee. Stephanie hid her smirk. At least he wasn't complaining.

It seemed as if it took forever to line up the participating boats and set sail in Santa Barbara bay. They'd head toward Stearns Wharf, sail around the end and along the other side, then down the coast for a few miles before starting back toward the harbor.

The magnificent sight of a fleet of decorated boats reflecting off the blackening sea made Stephanie's eyes prickle again. When she looked back toward shore and saw the rolling hillsides and houses heavily covered with holiday lights, and the palm tree silhouettes dotting the beach, she couldn't hold back her feelings. For the first time since Justin's death she'd explore the goodness of the season. She couldn't bring him back, but she could celebrate his short existence by refusing to let the sadness dictate her life. Even if it was only for tonight.

Overwhelmed, she let her tears brim and dribble down her cheeks. They weren't the usual tears that burned with guilt. Not today. They were tears of joy and goodwill…and letting go. Today she'd extend that goodwill to herself. A huge weight the size of Santa's gift sack seemed to lift from her shoulders. Suddenly feeling as buoyant as the ocean, she anchored herself to the rail and waved to the passing judges' motorboat, her smile genuine and filled with the spirit of the season.

Jason released the cork from the champagne bottle in his living room, sending it flying through the air as everyone ducked. While he splashed the bubbling liquid into several outreaching glasses, he beamed with satisfaction.

"Here's to a well-deserved win," he said. "We finally did it!"

Everyone cheered.

Phil saw Stephanie standing beside Claire and René, applauding along with everyone else.

The sight of her earlier on the boat had knocked him off balance. He'd felt compelled to make things right, but wasn't sure if she wanted anything to do with him, and he wanted to respect her feelings. He hadn't felt that lacking in confidence and confused over a woman since high school. All he knew for sure was that she'd left abruptly a week ago, and he hadn't been the same since. And that damn ticking clock counting down the days until she left for home didn't help either.

Under the bright lights of the Rogerses' family room, Stephanie's hair was decidedly red. The royal-purple satin blouse she wore accented the color even more. She'd taken off her ridiculous sweater, and he definitely liked what he saw.

He'd miss her when she was gone. Hell, he'd

missed her all week. She'd stay here until the first of the year, and if he played his hand right, he'd get things back on track and hopefully have her back in his bed before the night was over.

He snagged an extra glass of bubbly and delivered it to her. "Here's to our win."

Her bright eyes widened and her generous smile let him know she was happy to see him. "And kudos to you for juggling two squirming kids all evening."

He shook his head. "Man, since Robbie has been sleeping with CPAP he has even more energy. I was ready to throw him overboard a couple of times, but I kept thinking Roma would be really mad at me."

She laughed. "You'd never do that."

"Figure of speech." He enjoyed the little patches of red on her cheeks and neck. He'd spent enough time around her to know that meant she was nervous. He still made her nervous. Was that a good thing? Hell, she made him nervous, too, and he liked it.

"Admit it, you love that kid," she said.

"He is my brother." Talking about kids wasn't exactly what he had in mind. He'd had a whole week to devise his plan. "Can I talk to you for a minute?" With his hand on her lower back, he guided her to a quiet corner of the room.

"What's up?" She gazed at him with suspicion.

"We're friends, right? And we're supposed to be honest with each other," he said, noticing her eyes soften at the edges and her lusciously alluring lips pout ever so slightly. He wanted to kiss her, but they were in a room full of fellow employees. Even though whispers and suspicions traveled the watercooler circuit at the clinic, he wasn't about to flaunt their private relationship. "That's why I want you to know that I'm ready to take the next step."

Wide-eyed disbelief had returned. She took a quick sip of champagne and nearly choked on it. He tapped her back as her eyes watered.

"Sorry, didn't mean to shock you."

She coughed and sputtered. "What are you talking about—take the next step?"

"Listen," Phil said. "I know it's kind of hard to take a man dressed in a surfin' Santa suit seriously, but I want you to know I've really been doing a lot of thinking over the last week."

The suspicious glint returned to her eyes.

"Yeah, and the thing is I've decided to try commitment out."

"What?" She blurted a laugh. "Just like that? You're putting me on."

"Well, maybe one step at a time. Seriously, don't you think that's progress for a guy like me?"

"Hey, that's great. Really, I think it's great," she said, but the subtle slope of her shoulders and that naggingly suspicious gaze wasn't very encouraging. She obviously didn't believe he'd changed a bit.

"So you have any plans tomorrow?" he said.

The champagne flute was halfway to her mouth when she tossed him a surprised glance.

"I thought I'd hit the local shelter. Maybe you can help me pick out a dog?"

Bad timing. She'd taken another sip, and along

with her wry laugh she blew champagne out of her mouth.

"What? You don't think I can handle a committed relationship with a dog?"

All she could do was shake her head and point her finger at him with a one-day-I'll-get-you-back-for-this glower.

He knew he was pushing the limit, but he couldn't help playing with her, especially when her reaction was so satisfying. "What do you say, are you in?"

Having wiped her mouth, and found her voice again, she said, "I wouldn't miss that for the world."

What had gotten into Phil? He'd brought her a glass of champagne and strung her along with his newfound wisdom about relationships, then got her good. She shook her head and laughed to herself. The guy was completely spontaneous, and she thoroughly enjoyed him. She pushed aside the quick thought about love she'd had earlier.

He was ready to commit…to a dog.

She couldn't very well leave him to his own resources over such a big decision. The guy— the charming and sexiest Santa she'd ever laid her eyes on—needed help choosing a dog. How could she refuse?

Phil had hoped to bring Stephanie home with him tonight, but he didn't want to blow any progress he'd made by imposing his desires. He'd have to wait another day, get her all worked up over some canine's big brown eyes, have her help him make the dog at home then ask her to stay for dinner. If things worked out the way they usually did when the two of them were alone together, he'd put Fido in the yard and bring Stephanie back to his bed.

Not that he was using a dog simply to impress Stephanie. Once he'd thought about it and made the decision, he really wanted one. Loyal. Dependable. Warm. Loving. A dog would never leave him, and was exactly what he needed for companionship.

Phil turned the final corner to his street, rubbed

his jaw, and smiled. Being Santa had been a blast. Who could have guessed? If Stephanie hadn't pushed him into the job, he never would have known. And the constant smile on her face on the boat made all the humiliation worthwhile.

Something seemed different about her, he thought as he parked in his garage. He'd never been known for being intuitive, but he could have sworn she'd left half of her usual baggage behind tonight.

He'd picked up on her playful spirit and tested out the limits. He shook his head and grinned as he unlocked his house door. He'd imagined Stephanie Bennett doing all kinds of sexy things, but he'd never expected to see her spit champagne across the room. A hearty laugh tumbled from his throat as he stepped inside. It echoed off the empty house walls, and once again he was reminded how big and lonely his bachelor pad was.

The rows of metal cages, with every size, breed, and shape of dog filling every single one, almost broke Stephanie's heart. She could hardly bear to look into any of the dogs' eyes. The cages lined the walls of the cement-floored warehouse/shelter, where the smell of urine and dog breath permeated the air.

"I wish I could buy all of them," Phil said, echoing her sentiments.

His sincerity had her reaching for his hand.

He squeezed her fingers and gave her a tender glance. "This is going to be harder than I thought."

On the drive over, on a gorgeous sunny day, they'd discussed the kind of dog he was looking for—big, sleek and muscular. To Stephanie's ears his "kind of dog" sounded a bit like him. If she had her choice, she'd go for something petite and furry. Hmm, was that like her?

Loud barking and yipping made it almost impossible to carry on a conversation as they walked the length of the shelter. Some jumped and yipped incessantly, others hovered in the corners of their cages, and still others paced restlessly back and forth with anxious eyes taking everything in.

"Lots of these dogs got left behind when home owners walked away from their mortgages. With the lousy economy, other people couldn't afford to have a dog anymore," the shelter worker said. "We're hoping the Christmas season will help find some of these dogs homes."

Stephanie spotted a little bundle of cream-colored wavy fur with round brown eyes getting overrun by two other small dogs. It looked like a puppy.

The shelter worker must have picked up on her interest. "That one is a terrier mix. She's a bit older than most of the others."

"Hey, look at this one!" Phil called her attention away, but she glanced over her shoulder one last time at the so-called older dog, before moving on.

Amidst several cages of Labrador retrievers and German shepherds was a medium-size dark-furred dog.

"That one's a collie-Lab mix. One year old. Owner had to move out of state."

Phil petted the dog on his head, and the dog licked his hand.

"Both breeds are smart and they generally have good dispositions. Mixed breeds are often healthier than purebreds, too. They love their owners. Very loyal."

As if it was the easiest decision in the world, Phil nodded and smiled. "What's his name?"

"Daisy."

"It's a her, huh?"

"And she's been spayed."

"Good to know. Hey, Daisy, you like big yards and sunset walks along the beach?" The dog whimpered and licked his hand again.

Stephanie laughed at Phil's ability to charm females of all species.

"What do you think, Steph? Would Daisy and I make a good pair?"

His willingness to open his home to a forgotten pound dog warmed her insides. The change in his attitude since taking care of Robbie was astounding. She had the urge to give him a big kiss and hug, but touched his face instead. He hadn't shaved that morning, and the stubble made a scraping sound as she ran her fingers down his jaw.

"I think you and Daisy will make a great couple, and I promise I won't get jealous about your new female friend."

He smiled and nodded. "Then I'll take her."

As he filled out the paperwork and paid the fees, Stephanie kept going back to the little terrier mix up front. "Hey, sweetie," she whispered. The dog timidly explored the front of the cage, trying to sniff her fingers but not letting her touch his head. There seemed to be a world of sadness in his eyes. "You need a home, huh?"

"We'll take this one, too," Phil said from over her shoulder.

"What are you doing?" she said, rounding on him.

"I know love at first sight when I see it." He gave a magnanimous grin. "Consider him a Christmas present."

"I can't have a dog—I'm living in a hotel."

"The dog can stay with me until you go home. You have a town house in the desert, right?"

"Yes, but I…"

"Hey, don't analyze everything. Let's save two dogs today." Before she could respond, he looked for the shelter worker again. "What's this one's name?"

"Sherwood."

He laughed. "Sherwood. There you go. Stephanie and Sherwood. Sounds like a match made in heaven."

"How old is he?" she asked.

"He's older. Seven. His owner passed away."

That cinched it. The dog was grieving, something she understood completely. Though she felt inept, the shelter worker opened the cage and handed the dog to her. The trembling, compact dog fit perfectly in her arms. Fur partially covered soulful eyes, and a little pink tongue licked her knuckles. He was so trusting, and obviously missed his owner. The thought tied a string around her heart and squeezed. Phil was on to something. Maybe caring for a dog was the perfect stepping-stone for her lagging confidence. She could do this. She could take care of one small dog.

"You'll keep her until I move home?"

"I've got enough room for six dogs in my yard. Let's do it. Come on."

With more warm feelings washing over her, she hugged him and the dog yipped.

"Okay, Sherwood. Looks like you've got yourself a new mommy," she said, holding the dog to her face and enjoying the tickly fur.

The warm feeling that had started at the animal shelter continued to grow as Stephanie spent the afternoon with Phil. They'd shopped for leashes and beds and the proper food for each breed and, most importantly, travel cages.

Now that they'd unloaded everything at Phil's house, Sherwood had timidly gone into his cage, almost as if it was a security blanket, and Stephanie tried to coax him out.

"Come on, sweetie. I won't bite," she said, down on her knees, head halfway into the cage. She reached for him and he let her hold him then licked her face again.

"Maybe you should carry him like that for a while, until he gets used to the new house," Phil said, his dog dancing around his feet.

She nodded, stirring that warm bowl of feelings brewing stronger and stronger for Phil. He'd been a prince today. For a guy who didn't know the first thing about committing to a woman, he sure had no problem bringing a dog home.

"I can't figure out why I never did this before," he said, petting Daisy's silky black-and-white fur.

"I guess you just needed a nudge."

As if they'd known each other all their lives, he kissed her while each of them held their new dogs. His warm and familiar mouth covering hers felt so right she hoped the day would never end.

And later, when he asked her to spend the night with him, and she followed him down the hall to his bedroom, she realized the best part of the day was only getting started.

CHAPTER NINE

THE next week went by in a whirlwind. Stephanie and Phil were inseparable. She'd go to his house every day after work: they'd walk the dogs; catch up on any leftover paperwork from the clinic; cook dinner; make passionate love; have breakfast together; and head back to work. By Thursday, Phil suggested they carpool.

A red flag waved in Stephanie's mind. Wasn't carpooling a thinly disguised assumption that she'd return to his house again that night? Why couldn't he come right out and ask her to move in with him? Was this how all of his "flings" progressed, him keeping a subtle barrier until he tired of the woman and quit finding ways to spend time with her?

She only had two more weeks in Santa Barbara—did she really need to complicate her stay by thinking in such a manner? If she'd mentally agreed to "a fling," why were her emotions lagging so far behind?

Giving herself a silent pep talk, she agreed to drive to work with him then mentally ran down the pros and cons of her decision. This was a fling—an unbelievably wonderful fling with a guy who made her happy in all respects, a guy who never asked questions or made demands.

"You think this carpool business is a good idea?" she asked.

"It's good for the environment." He grinned.

She shook her head and rolled her eyes.

"You're already staying here every night. Sherwood wants you around." He glanced across the front seat at her then quickly back to the road. "I kind of like having you around."

This from a guy who supposedly didn't like to get involved or commit to relationships. She really needed to get her mind straight over this fling business.

"What are you really asking me, Phil?"

He pulled into his assigned parking place at the

clinic and parked then turned toward her with an earnest expression. "Since our time together is limited, I'm asking you to spend as much of it as possible with me." He reached for her hand and rubbed his thumb across her knuckles, igniting warm tingling up her wrist to the inside of her elbow. "We should explore this thing we've got going on."

So that was it. They had a "thing." Well, heck, she'd known they had a *thing* since the first time they'd kissed.

That red flag waved again. *He wants to have you in his bed every night, not have you move in or get involved or anything. He knows your time is limited. It gives him freedom to do whatever he wants with you...knowing you'll leave after Christmas.*

"Talk to me," he said. "I can see a million thoughts flying around your mind. Share one of them with me." His voice was husky and sincere. "Please."

She took a deep breath. "This is all so new to me. I guess I just need to know the rules."

"I'm the king of no strings, Steph. I think you know that."

She hesitated with a long inhalation. "No strings. Right."

Their eyes met and fused. For long silent moments they searched each other's souls for the truth. She wasn't positive what she read in his stare other than it made her feel dizzy and fuzzy-headed. She wasn't ready to tell him that it was too late, she'd probably fallen a little in love with him. How silly of her to think that. Love wasn't something you could do a little of. Love was like being pregnant—you either were or you weren't. Was she in love?

Hell, she'd really messed up with this fling thing. Next time, if there ever was a next time, she'd sit on the sidelines and leave it to the experts. Like Phil. He knew how to keep a sexy and satisfying relationship in its place. Just do it. Have a good time. Don't make any promises. Maybe it was a surfer's creed: ride the wave for all it's worth then move on to the next.

Apparently, Stephanie didn't have the no-strings gene.

Phil put his hand on the back of her head and pulled her toward him. His kiss was tender and meltingly warm. He kissed her as if he loved her, but that was her interpretation, her head was mixing everything up again. She'd blame it on being hormonal and still waiting for her period.

What he offered and what she felt were two different things. She needed to remember that. He only wanted her for two more weeks.

His lips kept nudging her, asking her to give back, to kiss him as if she meant it. She couldn't resist another second. Whatever words he'd just avoided saying, he communicated beautifully with his lips. I. Want. You. With. Me.

Did she need to know anything more than that?

As predicted on the previous night's news, the storm front moving down from Alaska had worked its way along the coast, first bringing gray skies, clouds, and cold temperatures on Thursday night, and by Friday morning, a week before Christmas Eve, full-out rain.

As the morning wore on, Stephanie became aware of something worse than stormy weather—nausea. Realizing exactly where she stood with Phil—nowhere!—had affected her more than she'd thought.

She sat with a new patient in her office. As she calculated the pregnant woman's expected due date, it hit her. Her hand trembled to the point of being unable to write.

She cleared her throat and verbally gave the due date, then used her best acting skills to hide the anguish brewing in her heart. "Congratulations. You'll have a late-summer baby. August, to be precise."

The young woman clapped her hands and beamed with joy. The complete opposite of how Stephanie felt. A late-summer baby?

The instant she'd ushered the ecstatic woman from her office, she got out the lab kit and drew a vial of blood from her arm, labeled it with a bogus name, and hand carried it to the laboratory for a STAT test.

After lunch, spent sitting in the darkness of her office, Stephanie frantically flipped through her reports, looking for the single most important lab of her life. She knew it was preposterous. She'd had her tubes tied! What were the odds? They certainly weren't in her favor—she'd looked it up—three different times. But defying the odds, she'd missed her period and showed early signs of pregnancy with fatigue, tender breasts, and mild nausea. It simply couldn't be!

With dread and a trembling hand, she continued to skim through the reports, and after a few more, there it was—her pregnancy blood test—and it was positive.

Her stomach protested as if she'd taken a five-hundred-foot free fall. Her pulse surged. She couldn't breathe. Her body switched to fight-or-flight mode.

She surged from the chair and strode toward the door on unsteady legs, her footsteps soon turning to a jog. She reached the clinic entry in a full sprint and just as she saw Phil on the periphery of her vision, she sprang outside and down the street, through the icy, pouring rain.

With all systems on automatic panic, she ran without a destination, unaware of the weather. She ran from her breaking point, she ran in a futile attempt to keep her sanity, her only goal to prolong the inevitable, to avoid the truth—she was pregnant.

"Stephanie, come back here!"

What in hell was she doing running down the street? Didn't she know it was practically hailing?

Phil raced down the sidewalk, slipped in a puddle, and nearly crashed into a bush. He recovered his balance, knocked a rolling trashcan out of his way then hurdled another, all while keeping Stephanie in his sight.

Not waiting for the streetlight, she crossed Cabrillo Boulevard, recklessly dodging a car, and headed for Stearns Wharf.

He didn't have a clue what had made her snap

and take off for the pier in a storm like this, but he sure as hell planned to catch up and find out, if she didn't get herself killed first!

She'd reached the beach, and headed for the pier. It may not have been such a great move, clearly not well thought out, but he had no choice. If he wanted to catch her, he'd have to tackle her, and finally he got close enough. He lunged and brought her down with a mild thud onto the wet sand.

She rolled onto her back, squealing. "What are you doing? Are you crazy?"

"I'm not the one sprinting between cars in the rain, darlin'," he panted. "Now, are you going to tell me what's going on?"

"Let go of me." She squirmed to break free.

"Not gonna happen. Calm down and talk to me." He pinned her arms above her head.

She sighed like an outsmarted teenager, wagging her head back and forth. Her tears blended with the rain. "I'm pregnant."

A rocket left his chest, headed straight toward his head, and exploded. The shock waves zapped every ounce of strength left his hands. "What? You're what?"

"I'm pregnant!"

"But your tubes are tied!"

She glanced up at him. "See? There's a reason I was running."

He sat back on his knees, raking his hands through his soaked hair. His vision blurred from the combination of rain and disbelief.

"I'm kicking myself for tackling you." He hopped up, pulling her up with him, before he spit out some sand. He couldn't leave her floundering on the beach. "Come here." He drew her into his rain-drenched arms, into a gritty, sand-wrapped hug. "What do we do now?" He felt her trembling and wondered, coupled with his jarring reaction, how much he was contributing to it.

"I can't have this baby." She wouldn't look him in the eyes. She kept shaking her head.

"I know you don't do kids, but maybe this is a good thing. Maybe you can get beyond that hang-up now."

"No!"

"Okay. Maybe just give yourself time to think this over."

"You don't understand." She sounded tormented.

Maybe he'd been too wrapped up in his own reaction. Sure, he was shocked, but the craziest thing followed—he wasn't upset about it. She obviously had an issue about the pregnancy, hence the jogging on the beach in the pouring rain. This was all new territory for him, too. He needed to handle her delicately, find out what she was thinking—because he cared. He gave a big fat damn about her and her feelings, and, most importantly, about the baby they'd made. "Try me. Tell me why you can't have this kid."

She tried to pull away, but his strength had returned and he didn't let her.

"Let me go!"

"No!" He clenched his teeth and fought to keep her near. "Tell me why you don't want the baby."

"I killed my baby." She spit out the words as if they were poison.

"What?" His pulse paused; a distant rumble of thunder helped jump-start it. "I don't believe that."

"I killed him. I let him fall." Her head drooped so low, he could barely hear her.

Lightning snapped and forked into branches over the ocean. Her confession deserved wisdom that he didn't have, but he wanted more that anything to do right by her. He'd never experienced anything close to this new-found desire in his life.

"Let's sit down. Get out of this rain." He led her to the covered bus stop a few feet away by the porpoise fountain. "Tell me what happened. I want to know everything." He took her by the shoulders and forced her to look at him. "You've got to tell me."

"You'll hate me when you find out."

"No. I won't." And he meant it. By God, he meant it.

She paced within the small confines of the bus stop as if she was a panicked animal, gulping her tears, gasping her words.

"Justin was a super-colicky baby. He never grew out of it. He was four months old and this time he'd cried three nights in a row. You have no idea how terrible it feels not to be able to console your child." She shuddered, and he fought the urge to wrap her in his arms for fear she'd quit talking.

"No matter what I did, he wouldn't calm down. I paced and sang. I rubbed his back. I gently bounced him. I walked and walked…all night long."

She hiccuped for air, hugged herself, hysteria emanating from her eyes. He wanted to console her, but couldn't fathom how. No wonder she'd freaked out with Robbie that first night.

"My arms ached. My back throbbed. I was exhausted. No matter how long I walked, no matter how I held him, sang to him, kissed him, he kept crying. Then finally the crying stopped. Justin had calmed down and gone to sleep in my arms. I didn't know what to do. If I moved he might start up again."

She spoke as if reliving the moment—locked in another time and place. Phil knew she couldn't have killed her baby. He knew there was a logical explanation, one she couldn't accept.

"If I put him in his crib I knew for certain he'd wake up. I eased onto the couch and he kept sleeping on my chest. So peaceful. So beautiful. For the first time in hours I found comfort. Comfort in the feel of my precious baby in my arms, and comfort for my aching back, my burning, sleepy eyes. I laid my head against the cushions and my son's gentle breathing lulled me to sleep."

A feral flash in her eyes alerted him that the hysteria was back. "I fell asleep!" she said, pain contorting her face. She continued her story as if he wasn't there. "I fell asleep," she sobbed. "And the next thing I knew… Oh, God, my baby!"

She dissolved into tears, crumpled to the bench. Phil rushed to lift her, to hold her up, to embrace her. After she settled down a bit he cupped her shoulders and stared into her eyes. "Tell me, sweetheart. Tell me everything."

She hiccuped another sob. "Justin fell off my chest, he fell off the couch, and…" She cried so hard she heaved, fluids pouring from every orifice on her face. She wiped her eyes with her palms, even as she cried more. "He hit his head on the table…"

Phil had never heard a woman cry like this in his life. He'd never seen such primal torture. He'd never imagined the depth of pain ripping at her.

"It damaged his brain." Then, as if finally giving in to the nightmare, her shoulders slumped in total defeat. "He died the next day."

Phil held her so tight he worried she might not be able to breathe, but she held him back, all trembles and shivers. "I never got to say good-bye, Phil," she whimpered, collapsing against his chest.

"Baby. Oh, honey. No. No, it wasn't your fault. Who let you believe it was your fault?" He pulled back to look at her. She avoided his eyes. "You weren't a single mother. Your man should have helped. You shouldn't have had to do it all your-self. Don't you see, he should have been there for you." Feeling anger at the bastard who'd let her down, Phil kissed her cheek.

They held each other tight for several minutes.

What the hell should he do now? A maelstrom of emotions, fears, and doubts knocked him off balance. He could only imagine how Stephanie felt. She thought she'd killed her baby, didn't deserve to ever be a mother again, had had her tubes tied to make sure she never would be, and still wound up pregnant.

And he was the father.

He didn't know what else to do, so he put his sopping wet jacket over their heads, and escorted Stephanie back to the clinic. When they got close, he flipped open his cell phone and called Jason as he steered Stephanie away from the clinic and toward his car.

"Jase, I'm taking Stephanie home. She's not feeling well."

Phil undressed Stephanie. She'd slipped into a stupor, trembling from the cold. He was in near shock, too, but one of them needed to function. He turned on the shower and waited for it to heat up then thrust her inside. She gasped, but didn't fight him.

He ripped off his wet and gritty clothes and climbed in with her, easing her head under the water, making sure her body warmed up.

"Come on, honey, turn around. Let the water hit your back." The steamy shower felt good. He dipped his head under the stream and shook it.

What in the hell were they supposed to do now?

Sherwood and Daisy came sniffing around the bathroom, obviously aware that something wasn't right.

With Stephanie still out of it, Phil tried to gather his thoughts. He'd never been in this position before. He watched her through the water. She stared blankly at the tile. His heart ached for her. He could only imagine the torture she'd lived through, the guilt, the self-hatred, and now her hibernating nightmare had been reawakened.

He washed her hair and lathered his own. The excess sand and mud gathered around the drain.

"Are you warmer now?"

She didn't respond.

"Let's get you dried off then I'll put you to bed."

Her worst fear may have materialized, except there was one thing different this time around.

He was the father.

CHAPTER TEN

PHIL bundled a second blanket over Stephanie, but she still trembled. He made a snap decision to share his body warmth, and climbed under the covers then spooned up against her. She snuggled into his hold. Heavy rain sounded like Ping-Pong balls on the roof, and crackles of thunder in the distance made the cuddling even more intimate.

After the shower, he'd blow-dried and brushed her hair, and now it splayed across the pillow, tickling his face. It seemed odd to smell his standard guy shampoo in her hair instead of the usual flowers-and-dew-scent shampoo she used. Up on one elbow, he pushed the waves away from her shoulder and dropped a kiss on her neck.

"We'll get through this, Steph," he whispered.

They'd leaped a thousand steps ahead in their

relationship with today's news. What should they do? He'd just finished a crash course on parenting with Robbie and had barely made the grade, but this was different. They'd made a baby. Together. Was he ready for this?

And what about Stephanie? The last thing in the world she wanted was a child. He'd never been in this position before. One thing was certain; he didn't want to run away from the challenge. A part of him was excited about being a father.

A swell of tender feelings made Phil pull her closer. He pressed another kiss to that special spot on her shoulder.

Stephanie needed oblivion. She needed to find one tiny corner of her mind and hide there. She didn't want to think. Couldn't bear the truth.

A vague memory of Phil bathing and drying her then brushing her hair filled her heart with gratitude. Even in her haze, she could sense the delicate way he'd treated her. Now his warm hands surrounded her and pulled her close. His breath caressed her neck. He kissed her…there. Chills fanned across her breasts and she suddenly knew how to keep from thinking about anything but Phil.

She turned into his arms and eager mouth. His kiss was different. The passion was still there, but this one felt warmer than all the others had. Phil handled her gently, lovingly, taking their kisses slowly, yet building each on the next until she longed for more of him. She needed his hands touching her everywhere, and guided one to her breast. He didn't require schooling on the rest. She cupped his head at her chest as he kissed and taunted her. Desire burrowed through her, down to her belly.

As his arms explored and caressed every part of her, her legs entwined with his locking him tight. With his passion obvious, she moved against him, placing him at her entrance. His hand moved between them, touching and teasing her, making her squirm for more. She needed to forget everything, and Phil's deep kisses and sex would soothe all the aching in her soul.

His tongue delved into her mouth as he simultaneously entered her with a slow, determined thrust. She gasped as she stretched and gloved him. He kissed her harder and quickened his rhythm, the building heat pulsing through her center. Her inner muscles throbbed as he edged farther inside. His breathing went rough and ragged and he cupped and tilted her hips for deeper access. She gulped for air and ground against his powerful penetration, her muscles and nerves winding tighter and tighter with every lunge.

He held her at the peak of pleasure with the steady pace, and she thrived on every sensation swirling through her body. She never wanted the exquisite feeling to end and, languishing there with her, it seemed his only desire was to please her. Feeding on the suspended moments of bliss, her hunger grew. He'd made her frantic and dependent on him to take her all the way. As if reading her thoughts, he doubled his rhythm, pushing and nudging her to the brink, holding her there until she begged for release and he erupted.

Tears streamed down her cheeks as she quivered and gave in to the pulsations pounding through her body, floating her outside of time and mind and, like a heavy sedative, numbing her to harsh reality.

Phil had taken her there—to oblivion.

Stephanie cracked open an eye. The room was still dark. She'd been sleeping, one glance at the bedside clock told her, for hours. Phil breathed peacefully beside her, his warmth like a snug cocoon. Sherwood had curled into a ball at the foot of the bed, and Daisy sprawled out on a nearby rug.

The snapshot of domestic tranquility shocked her back into the moment.

An odd fragment of thought repeated itself in her mind. *Who let you believe it was your fault? You weren't a single mother. Your man should have helped. You shouldn't have had to do it all yourself. Don't you see, he should have been there for you.*

She blinked and sat up as the course of the afternoon came roaring back through her mind. Phil rustled and turned. She studied him. Had he said those words merely to console her or did he really believe them?

Was a guy like Phil capable of committing to one woman? Would it matter if he could? She shook her head—she couldn't handle this pregnancy. She never deserved to be a mother again.

She lay back on the pillow and stared through the shadows at the ceiling, desperately in need of sorting through her problems.

She studied Phil's mop of dark blond hair, his straight and strong profile. She ran her finger along the length of his red-tinged sideburn. In other circumstances, she could see herself waking up next to a guy like Phil for the rest of her life. If things were different.

It was a fool's dream.

You don't deserve to be happy. You're a murderer.

Out of reflex, she curled into a ball and covered her eyes. The negative thoughts her husband had charged her with day after day until they'd divorced became so strong she couldn't ward them off. A queasy feeling took hold in her stomach, and self-hatred pulled her deeper inward. She definitely couldn't keep the baby.

"Are you all right?" Phil took her by the shoulders and shook her. "Hey, what's going on? Are you having a nightmare?" He pulled her to him and kissed the top of her head.

"Yes," was all she could whisper. "A nightmare."

"Come here," he said, rubbing her back and kissing her again.

He wanted to protect her. Had her ex-husband ever offered to protect her at the worst moment of her life? No. He'd blamed her. He'd called her out as the monster she was.

What kind of person would do that? he'd accused.

Along with the vivid memory, Stephanie whimpered, and Phil drew her closer to him. His warm chest and strong arms gave little solace. She didn't deserve solace.

"Let me take care of you," he said. 'I don't want anything bad to happen to you."

What happened to two weeks of good times? No strings attached? Now, only because she was pregnant, he wanted to take care of her? If she weren't pregnant, would he still want her? Could she trust a man like Phil to be there if she needed him?

He was practically a stranger, and she needed to think things through.

Confused and unable to respond to his caring words, she bolted from the bed.

He looked like a man about out of patience.

"Phil…" She paced the length of the rug. "This wasn't supposed to happen with us."

"You're right. But it did, and now we have to figure out what to do."

Why did he sound so reasonable?

The jumble of feelings and fears caused that queasy sensation to double into a fist of nausea. Before she could think another thought, she sprinted for the bathroom.

Phil sat outside the washroom door, listening to Stephanie heave as if exorcising a demon. He scrubbed his face. What in hell was he supposed to do now? Was he anywhere near ready to be a father? At the moment it seemed the bigger problem was that Stephanie felt determined *not* to be a mother again.

What kind of mind game had her ex-husband played on her to make her feel so unworthy of a second chance?

Behind the door, the toilet flushed and the faucet was turned on. For Stephanie's fragile sake, no matter how much he wanted to, he wouldn't dare broach the subject that *they* were having a baby until she brought it up.

Maybe he could distract her. Why not pretend things were the same as they were two days ago? What normal activity would they have done this weekend before everything had changed?

"I was thinking that maybe today we could shop for a Christmas tree," he called through the door, feeling completely at a loss for what to say or do. All he knew was that he wanted to make things easier for her. Maybe he could distract her with something fun and frivolous like buying a Christmas tree. It was the season.

She didn't answer.

Lame idea. Okay, he'd think of something else. He'd help her get through the shock of it by keeping her busy, and maybe in the process he'd manage to work out his own feelings. "Or we could take the dogs to the beach."

Still no answer.

A few minutes later, she emerged from the bathroom fully dressed.

He went on alert.

"I'm going away," she said. "I need to be alone."

He jumped to his feet. "What? Don't I figure into this?"

With eyes as flat as stone, she looked at him. "Ultimately, it all comes down to me and what I decide to do."

He words were like a slap to the face. Just like that, she'd shut him out. He needed to buy time, to keep her there. "At least let me fix you something to eat."

"I don't want anything."

"You can't just think about yourself anymore." Ah, damn, that had been the wrong thing to say. Why was he such an idiot?

She gave him a measured look. He wished he could see inside her mind, to figure out what was going on. He was at a loss and she wasn't having a thing to do with his fumbling attempts to keep her there.

Stunned silent, he watched her gather up her purse and leave.

Phil couldn't stand staying in his house alone, so he herded the dogs into his Woodie and drove to the beach. Sherwood stayed close to his side as Daisy romped through the waves, chasing the Frisbee he threw again and again.

Never in his life had he been more confused about a woman. He'd covered for his true feelings when he'd insisted they carpool to work together. He hadn't wanted to scare her off by asking her to move in with him for the rest of her time in Santa Barbara, though that was exactly what he'd wanted. Hell, these new feelings scared him enough for both of them. The problem was, for the first time in his adult life he was open to exploring where this "thing" between him and Stephanie might lead. And she'd have nothing to do with him.

He'd never cherished a woman in his life, yet last night, after she'd told him her darkest secret and they'd made love, he'd felt the subtle shift of his heart. She'd transformed from hot girlfriend to the woman he loved…and she was carrying their child. Had he just admitted he loved her?

He swallowed, wanting nothing more than to prove he could be the kind of man she deserved. A man who believed in her, who'd never let her down. Was he capable of such a thing?

He'd learned an important fact about himself when Robbie had been thrust on him. When he set his mind to something, he could do it. No matter how foreign or hard, he could make it work. He and his little brother were closer than ever before, and Phil was quite sure he could do even better by his own kid. The thought excited him, and he wanted to make things work out with Stephanie. He'd never wanted anything so much in his life.

Yet, just like his mother, when life had gotten tough, she'd split.

Daisy scampered toward him, soaking wet, and dropped the slobbery Frisbee at his feet. Deep in thought, he hardly noticed he'd thrown the toy back to sea. Sherwood snuggled on his lap. Without thinking, he rubbed the dog's ears.

"Don't worry, boy, she'll be back for you. I'm the one she left."

Phil couldn't sleep all weekend. He felt like hell on Monday, and with a million lectures planned for Stephanie, he was surprised to find out she'd called in sick. As hard as it was, he'd given her the weekend to sort things through, but she still wasn't ready to face him. Or their baby.

Frustrated, he scraped the stubble on his jaw. Damn, he'd forgotten to shave, but it didn't matter. He was far more concerned whether Stephanie had made a rash decision or not. Damn it, he deserved to be in on *any* decisions she made about their baby, but she wouldn't answer her phone. He'd called by the extended-stay hotel, only to be told she'd checked out.

He dialed her cell number again and it went directly to messages, then he shoved it back into his pocket. Gaby give him a strange look.

"What?" he said.

"Nothing." She went back to her task as if it was the most important thing on the planet.

Jason buzzed him on the intercom. "Hey, just wanted to tell you that Claire is going to pick up as many of Stephanie's patients as she can. I'll see a few myself."

"I'm a pulmonologist." Phil censured the expletive he wanted to utter. "I don't know squat about gynecology. Can't help." He clicked off without giving Jason a chance to respond.

Stephanie cried about everything. What to eat. What to wear. Whether to get out of bed. Whether to run away to the desert. Every single thing about life set her off.

She'd changed hotels, and gave strict instructions

that no one was to know which room she was in. Yet deep inside she wished Phil would find her. And that made her cry, too.

With each passing day, she grew more aware of the life forming inside her, and with that knowledge she forged a private bond with the baby. The thought of giving it up...made her cry.

She couldn't fight her desire to be in Phil's arms any more than she could resist his easy charm, so she'd opted to stay away. When she'd bared her soul to him, he'd acted more like a prince than a playboy. He'd gathered her close to his chest and stroked her cheek with his thumb, and she'd almost believed that things could work out for them. Almost.

She'd seen all the evidence over the past month. He'd professed to be a confirmed and happy bachelor, yet he owned a house fit for a family. He loved to putter around in the yard and garden just as much as he liked to surf. And he was a great cook, better than she was.

When she saw how he was with Robbie, she knew he'd make a great father for some lucky child some day. And when he'd suggested they each buy a dog, it had almost been as if he'd wanted to test the waters on commitment.

But that was her side of the story. What he really thought or felt would remain a mystery, because she couldn't face him. Not with what she had planned.

She sighed and pulled the comforter closer. Besides, he deserved a lady who wanted kids, and she'd finally made up her mind what she was going to do. And the decision…made her cry.

CHAPTER ELEVEN

STEPHANIE'S sense of duty drove her back to work on Wednesday. That and the fact she couldn't bear to be alone with her tortured thoughts another day.

She entered the MidCoast Medical clinic cautiously, peeked around the door and edged her way inside.

The first voice she heard was Phil's and she almost ran the other way. A fist-size knot clenched her stomach, forcing her to stand still.

"Gaby," he said, "I asked you to bring Mr. Leventhal in this morning. Why is he still on the schedule for this afternoon?" He sounded irritated.

"It didn't work with his schedule, Dr. Hansen." Smooth professional that she was, Gaby didn't let his snit bother her. "Welcome back, Dr. Bennett."

Stephanie had never seen Phil look so horrible. He had dark circles under his eyes similar to football players' black antiglare paint, and when was the last time the man had shaved? His hair was in need of a good combing, too, and…did he actually have on two different-colored socks?

He stopped in his tracks when he noticed her. She didn't look any better than he did. His consuming stare made her forget how to breathe. All she could do was nod and make a straight line for her office. She felt his glare on her back the entire way, and prayed he wouldn't follow her.

With a trembling hand, she reached for the doorknob. How would she make it through the day?

Feeling emotionally and physically drained, she wondered how much longer she could keep going like this. After the New Year, she'd move back to Palm Desert, but first she had to get through Christmas, and she owed the medical clinic the time she'd signed on for. After she put on her doctor's coat, she wrapped her hands around her waist and realized she'd been doing that a lot lately. The baby was quickly becoming a part of her every thought.

Maria Avila came waddling into the clinic. "My back is killing me," she said.

"Why don't you go home, take a load off your feet? You don't have to do this today," Stephanie said.

"Are you kidding? This is what I live for. If I go home, I'll have two kids under the age of five to chase around. Heck, I know where I'm better off." She gave a wry laugh, and her face lit up with her usual infectious grin. "Besides, I need to make up for that clinical day I missed on Thanksgiving."

Stephanie couldn't help but smile back as she shook her head. "Here's our first patient. Why don't you do the honors?" At least one of them wanted to be there.

Maria snatched the chart. "Great!"

All morning Maria shadowed Stephanie. Occasionally, she rubbed her back and sighed, but never complained about the highly charged pace Stephanie insisted on keeping. It was the only way to keep her mind off Phil and their baby.

At lunchtime, Stephanie holed up in her office with a sack lunch, and Maria waddled off to the nurses' lounge.

"I'm gonna go put my feet up," Maria said, on her way out of the office.

No less than five minutes later, just as Stephanie finished a small sandwich, a rapid knock alerted her to someone at the door. Her heart stammered, and she prayed it wasn't Phil.

The door swung inward as it became evident her prayer hadn't been answered. He closed it and strode toward her desk, his intense gaze knocking the wind out of her.

"Have you made up your mind yet about what you plan to do?"

She stared at her desk. There wasn't the slightest tone of compassion in his voice. He hadn't wasted one second on preliminaries. If he wanted to be direct, she'd join him. "I'm going to give the baby up for adoption."

* * *

Her decision hit Phil as if a boulder had dropped on his chest—it crushed him and made it hard to breathe. Give their baby up? He'd been on the verge of telling her he loved her the other morning, the day she'd left. She'd put him through hell this week while he impatiently waited for her to make her decision. Now she'd made the second-worst decision he could have imagined. Give up their baby?

Could he honestly love a woman who would walk away from her child? She wasn't an unwed teenager—she was a well-established adult who could easily care for a child. Yet she wanted to give the baby away. It didn't make any sense, but he'd never been in her shoes. He couldn't imagine how it must feel to bear the brunt of a child's accidental death.

He wanted more than anything to be angry at her for resisting this special gift, but he couldn't. The fact was he loved her. He wasn't sure if she felt anything for him, though. Her careless disregard for his feelings proved otherwise.

"The baby is mine, too. Remember?" he said. "We made it together."

She glanced at him, as if it had never occurred to her that he might want to be involved in the decisions.

He stood before her, hands at his sides, opening and closing his fists. "How selfish of you. You haven't even asked me what I'd do."

Surprise colored her eyes. She sat straighter. Had it really never occurred to her that he'd want to be involved with any decision she made about their baby? Things were more screwed up than he'd imagined.

"I'm sorry if that's what you think. Doesn't it always fall on the woman?" She stood and met him eye to eye. He fought the urge to grab her arms and shake her. "You've got your carefree life. You've never given me a hint that you were interested in anything more than sex and a good time, and suddenly I'm supposed to consult you because I got pregnant? Is that it?"

She'd challenged him, and he needed to tell

her the truth. If nothing else, she deserved the truth.

"The day I met you," he said, "I was really turned on by your looks, but the more I got to know you, the more I knew you'd been hurt in life. I just wanted to be your friend and, if I was lucky, maybe be your lover. I never would have dreamed what followed."

"That I'd screw things up and get pregnant?"

He ignored her defiant tone. "That I would fall in love with you."

Stephanie needed to sit down.

Tingles burst free in her chest and rained over her body. She squeezed her eyes closed, and soon large tears dripped over her cheeks. She clenched her jaw to keep from blubbering. If only she weren't pregnant, she'd be free to love him, too. "Phil..."

"I want you to know where I stand." He knelt in front of her and looked into her face. She bowed her head to hide her tears.

At a loss for one single word, Stephanie withdrew into her thoughts. She loved him; *he* loved her, so why couldn't they have a happy ending? Because she couldn't bear to lose another child— she still didn't trust herself.

"If you're giving up the baby," he said, "give it to me."

"Give it to you?" Oh, God, how could she do that? She loved Phil, and he wanted to keep their baby. Remembering the special love she'd felt from him last Friday night, and how he'd taken care of her like a mother hen, she believed he loved her, but would he want her if she wasn't pregnant? Now she'd lose both the baby and Phil. Could she remove herself so easily from the equation? If she changed her mind and wanted to keep the baby, would he want her, too? Or would he hate her?

"I'll do the best I can as a father."

She couldn't believe what he was telling her.

By putting him in this situation, not by choice, she'd never know if he stayed with her out of love or obligation, and not knowing for sure would kill her and eventually ruin their relationship. Oh,

God, her mind was so mixed up, she couldn't think straight.

"Please don't hate me, Phil. You can't understand…"

He shook his head and paced the floor. "Yes, losing your baby was a tragedy. I can't imagine how it must feel, but, Stephanie, you're alive, not dead, and you've got to let it go. That was three years ago. It's time to move on."

He was right, she knew he was right, but she was so damn stuck in her self-loathing rut…

Amy came rushing through the door. "Maria's water broke, and she's having contractions!"

Stephanie jumped to her feet, her legs having turned to rubber bands. Maria had gone into labor, as she'd been threatening for six weeks since Stephanie had first met her.

Words, as dry as the desert, crawled out of her mouth. "Have you called the paramedics?"

"She wants you, Doctor," Amy said, eyes huge from adrenaline.

She hadn't signed on for this. It said so in her contract—no delivering babies.

"Where is she?" Stephanie asked in a wobbling voice, following Amy to the procedure room.

Phil remained at her side, supporting her elbow and walking briskly with her. "You know what to do, and I'll be here, right here. We'll get through this together."

His words of encouragement meant more than she could say.

Stephanie rushed into the procedure room, where Amy had left Maria between contractions. Phil was right on her heels.

"Maria, do you think you can make it to the hospital?" Stephanie said.

"Feels like the kid's head is between my knees!"

Claire appeared. "I'm here if you need me." Word had traveled fast through the clinic.

Surrounded by her clinic family and Phil, Stephanie felt confidence spring back to life. She'd delivered more babies than she could count. She could do this. She went to the sink and splashed water on her face and washed her hands, then gowned up and gloved. "Let's have a look," she said.

This was Maria's third baby, the woman knew the drill.

She'd check for effacement, dilatation and station. "One hundred percent, ten centimeters, plus three. I guess your baby doesn't plan to wait for an ambulance," Stephanie said, her heart kicking up a couple notches on the beat scale.

Amy rushed around the room gathering everything they might possibly need.

Stephanie glanced over her shoulder at Phil, who was looking a little pale, but was still there.

He touched her arm and nodded. "You'll do fine. Now I'm going to step out of your way, but holler if you need me."

As if on cue, Maria let out a guttural sound.

Stephanie saw Maria's abdomen tighten into a hard ball. Now was the time to click into the moment and do what she'd been trained for. All other thoughts left her mind. Half an hour later, she positioned herself at the birth canal before giving a terse command. "Push!"

A tiny head with dark hair matted with vernix crowned.

"Keep pushing!" She slowly guided the baby's face-down head through the birth canal. "Okay, now stop pushing." She made a quick check to make sure the umbilical cord wasn't wrapped around the baby's neck. It wasn't. "Push. Push."

Soon the entire body flopped into her waiting hands, and the baby let out a wail.

Stephanie held the newborn as if he was made of porcelain. The squirming bundle of perfection mewed and tried to open his eyes. A booster shot of adrenaline made her hands shake. *What if I drop him?* Her arms felt as if they carried the weight of the world.

Phil appeared at her side, and put his gloved hands around the child for added support. His eyes met hers and she saw all the confidence she lacked right there. He believed in her. That look told her he knew she could do it. He'd never doubted her. He knew she could handle her own baby, too.

She bit her bottom lip to stop herself crying.

Hadn't she done enough of that lately? "It's a boy!" Emotionally wrung out, she held the baby close enough for Maria to see. "He's gorgeous."

Maria grinned and nodded in agreement as Stephanie laid the newborn on her stomach.

"May I?" Phil asked, snipping the umbilical scissors in the air.

"Be my guest," Maria said, cuddling her baby to her breast.

Phil glanced at Stephanie. "I wanted to get a little practice in before our baby arrives," he whispered into her ear, before severing the cord.

His words meant more than anything in the world just then.

After the placenta was delivered, and the ambulance arrived to transport Maria, Stephanie cleaned up and went back to her office. Phil was right at her side. His eyes were bright with the buzz from Maria's delivery as he closed the door.

"You were fantastic. You can handle anything you set your mind to," he said.

The high from the delivery had boosted her

confidence, and Phil's support meant every-thing to her. He stepped closer and touched her shoulder.

"We're going to have a baby. Steph. Look at me. In case you're wondering, I want you and I want our kid."

She gave him a questioning glance, her heart thumping so hard she thought it might crack a rib.

"I'm ready to make the leap," he said. "And it's all because of you, sweetheart."

If she'd ever doubted that he loved her, that doubt vanished. Even though he knew her tragic secret, he still loved her. He was the best man she'd ever met.

"Nothing will sway me. Now that I've discov-ered you, I can't let you go," he said. "I've fallen crazy in love with you." He took her into his arms. "I'm here to tell you I'm ready. I want you. You're the woman I love. But there's one thing that will hold us back, that is if you don't love me, too."

Why hadn't she told him? He'd opened his soul and she'd been wallowing in self-pity. He hadn't cursed her and run off when he'd found out she'd dropped her baby. He'd forced her to open her heart with small steps and a dog named Sherwood. He'd made love to her as if she were a goddess. He'd forced his way inside her fortress and conquered her heart. The guy deserved to know how she felt.

"I do. I love you, Phil. More than I can ever express."

A relieved grin stretched across his face and he covered her mouth with his, whispering over her lips, "It's about time you admitted it."

After he'd kissed her thoroughly, leaving her breathless and weak-kneed, he held her at arm's length.

"You need to forgive yourself. *Really* forgive yourself. Your ex-husband let you down. He was a jerk. These horrible things happen in life, and somehow we have to dig deeper and keep going.

"I love you and I promise to never let you down. And if I do, you have my permission to call me on it. I won't run. I won't hate you. I'll love and respect you. I'll always love you, Stephanie."

She crumpled into his embrace on another wave of tears, and he welcomed her with open arms. With the deepest feeling of connection to another human being she'd ever felt, she hugged him back.

They belonged together, both broken and jagged along the edges but a perfect fit. Filled with hope, she knew without a doubt that his unconditional love would finally help her heal.

"So what do we do now?" he said, against her ear.

She pulled back and gazed into his sea-blue eyes. As he'd said everything she needed to hear, and she had admitted exactly how she felt, there really wasn't much left to say or do. Except one silly thought popped into her mind. "Let's go and buy that Christmas tree."

His full-out laugh was the second-best sound she'd heard all day, the first having been the new-born baby's cry.

* * *

On Christmas Eve, Stephanie had come down with a mild cold. Phil insisted she stay in bed, but she didn't want to miss such a special holiday, her first Christmas with the man she loved.

Their decorated tree blinked and twinkled in the corner of the family room. A few gifts, mostly for the dogs, were wrapped and tucked beneath. Christmas carols played quietly in the background. The incredible aroma of roast beef filled the air as it cooked in the oven, along with Yorkshire pudding, making her mouth water.

Carl and Roma arrived with hyperactive Robbie. What was it about Christmas that got kids so wound up?

She grinned at the boy, and stooped to his level before he had a chance to tackle her. Her legs were still sore from Phil's tricky maneuver at the beach the week before, and Robbie's version of hugging was to throw his body against hers.

"Pill," Robbie said, quickly losing interest in Stephanie when he noticed his big brother.

"Dude!" Phil hugged him, and Stephanie had

to blink when he kissed his brother on the cheek. "Merry Christmas."

Robbie's gaze darted everywhere. "Wow, did Santa come to your house already?" He saw the gifts and ran for the tree.

Daisy and Sherwood intercepted him, hopping in circles and demanding their fair share of attention. Easily distracted, Robbie giggled and jumped around with them.

Stephanie grinned, thinking the dogs were protecting their doggy cookies and leather chews but knowing they loved any and all attention they could get. She watched Robbie roll around on the floor with them, and soon felt a hand on her shoulder.

It was Carl.

"Thank you," he said.

She looked into the same blue eyes she'd woken up to that morning, and imagined how Phil would look thirty years down the road. She liked what she saw.

"For what?" she said.

"For making my son happy. For helping him finally grow up."

She shook her head and hugged Carl. "He's done the same for me."

Christmas evening, one year later...

Stephanie sat bundled in a blanket and snuggling with Phil on the couch. She stared at the Christmas tree in the dimmed living room. It really was the most beautiful tree she'd ever seen. The decorations reflected the colorful blinking lights across the family-room ceiling, and the effect was nothing short of magical.

Their family and friends had come and gone and they were finally alone. She looked up at her husband, who bore a mischievous grin.

"I've got an idea how to make an already perfect day even better," he said. He dipped his head and kissed her neck, sending feathery tickles over her chest. She reached for him and kissed his jaw, enjoying the evening stubble and waning spice of his aftershave.

"That sounds wonderful," she whispered.

He stood, held her hands, and pulled her to her feet.

Baby gurgles and coos came through the nursery intercom. From their brand-new Santa-delivered dog beds, Daisy's and Sherwood's ears perked up.

Stephanie smiled at Phil. "Shall we wait to see how long before she realizes she's hungry?"

They looked at each other briefly and said in unison, "Nah."

Phil led her down the hall and together they peeked in on the center of their universe—their four-month-old daughter, Emma.

The contented baby lay on her back in her crib, reaching for the tiny stuffed animals dangling from the mobile over her bed. Her foot made contact with a teddy bear and she squealed with delight.

Stephanie and Phil laughed quietly. They loved watching her, and wanted to steal a few more moments enjoying the show before she noticed them. But it was too late. The baby glanced at the doorway and squealed even louder when she saw them. She flapped her arms and legs as if she might fly to them.

Stephanie rushed to her and lifted her into her arms, smothering her with kisses. Emma cooed and gurgled, and laughed. She'd reached a euphoric stage in her life, and everything seemed to make her happy.

Phil wrapped his arms around both Stephanie and Emma and hugged them tight. "How're my girls doing this Christmas night?"

Stephanie pressed her cheek to Emma's and glanced up at Phil as if she was posing for a picture. "Just fine, Daddy. We couldn't be happier."

MEDICAL™

Large Print

Titles for the next six months...

June

ST PIRAN'S: THE WEDDING OF THE YEAR	Caroline Anderson
ST PIRAN'S: RESCUING PREGNANT CINDERELLA	Carol Marinelli
A CHRISTMAS KNIGHT	Kate Hardy
THE NURSE WHO SAVED CHRISTMAS	Janice Lynn
THE MIDWIFE'S CHRISTMAS MIRACLE	Jennifer Taylor
THE DOCTOR'S SOCIETY SWEETHEART	Lucy Clark

July

SHEIKH, CHILDREN'S DOCTOR...HUSBAND	Meredith Webber
SIX-WEEK MARRIAGE MIRACLE	Jessica Matthews
RESCUED BY THE DREAMY DOC	Amy Andrews
NAVY OFFICER TO FAMILY MAN	Emily Forbes
ST PIRAN'S: ITALIAN SURGEON, FORBIDDEN BRIDE	Margaret McDonagh
THE BABY WHO STOLE THE DOCTOR'S HEART	Dianne Drake

August

CEDAR BLUFF'S MOST ELIGIBLE BACHELOR	Laura Iding
DOCTOR: DIAMOND IN THE ROUGH	Lucy Clark
BECOMING DR BELLINI'S BRIDE	Joanna Neil
MIDWIFE, MOTHER...ITALIAN'S WIFE	Fiona McArthur
ST PIRAN'S: DAREDEVIL, DOCTOR...DAD!	Anne Fraser
SINGLE DAD'S TRIPLE TROUBLE	Fiona Lowe

MILLS & BOON

MEDICAL™

Large Print

September

SUMMER SEASIDE WEDDING	Abigail Gordon
REUNITED: A MIRACLE MARRIAGE	Judy Campbell
THE MAN WITH THE LOCKED AWAY HEART	Melanie Milburne
SOCIALITE...OR NURSE IN A MILLION?	Molly Evans
ST PIRAN'S: THE BROODING HEART SURGEON	Alison Roberts
PLAYBOY DOCTOR TO DOTING DAD	Sue MacKay

October

TAMING DR TEMPEST	Meredith Webber
THE DOCTOR AND THE DEBUTANTE	Anne Fraser
THE HONOURABLE MAVERICK	Alison Roberts
THE UNSUNG HERO	Alison Roberts
ST PIRAN'S: THE FIREMAN AND NURSE LOVEDAY	Kate Hardy
FROM BROODING BOSS TO ADORING DAD	Dianne Drake

November

HER LITTLE SECRET	Carol Marinelli
THE DOCTOR'S DAMSEL IN DISTRESS	Janice Lynn
THE TAMING OF DR ALEX DRAYCOTT	Joanna Neil
THE MAN BEHIND THE BADGE	Sharon Archer
ST PIRAN'S: TINY MIRACLE TWINS	Maggie Kingsley
MAVERICK IN THE ER	Jessica Matthews

MILLS & BOON